MEPHISTO'S
WALTZ

—— STORIES ——

Sergio Pitol

Translated by George Henson

DEEP VELLUM PUBLISHING

DALLAS, TEXAS

Deep Vellum Publishing
3000 Commerce St., Dallas, Texas 75226
deepvellum.org · @deepvellum

Deep Vellum Publishing is a 501c3
nonprofit literary arts organization founded in 2013.

ISBN: 978-1-941920-83-1 (paperback) · 978-1-941920-81-7 (ebook)

Library of Congress Control Number: 2017938737

Cover design by Tanya Wardell
Typesetting by Kirby Gann · kirbygann.net

Text set in Bembo, a typeface modeled on typefaces cut by Francesco Griffo
for Aldo Manuzio's printing of De Aetna in 1495 in Venice.

Distributed by Consortium Book Sales & Distribution · (800) 283-3572 ·
cbsd.com
Printed in the United States of America on acid-free paper

TABLE OF CONTENTS

Introduction by Elena Poniatowska   vii

Victorio Ferri Tales a Tale   1

Like the Gods   9

The Panther   19

Body Present   25

Warsaw Bound   43

Westward Bound   53

The Return   65

Icarus   77

The Wedding Encounter   87

Tía Clara's Devices   113

Cemetery of Thrushes   121

Mephisto's Waltz   161

Bukhara Nocturne   179

The Dark Twin   207

THE ORIGIN OF SERGIO PITOL'S WORK

Here was a grandmother with her grandson; they lived on a hacienda of hot earth, of vanilla and spices, of reed beds and black vultures and roosters, all unbearable because of their insistence. The grandmother read books to the little boy who was ill from every kind of fever, tropical and literary, and, meanwhile, the little boy grew beneath the sheets, lanky, secret, malarial, complex, wide-eyed, curious, unhappy because he believed he had been denied happiness. This Renaissance child, ungraspable, charming, somnambulistic, apart, descendant of the Capulets and the Montagues but above all of the Deméneghi, the Buganzas, the Sampieri, and the Pitols.

While the grandmother read, Sergio Pitol began to live his own life of fantasy, and he never left it. Sergio never inhabited a reality that was not a part of literature. His journeys were a continuation of that never-ending tale spun by Catalina Deméneghi, his grandmother, whose thread began to unravel, taking him to the ends of the planet. Pitol arrived in Poland, beneath the earth's crust and emerged in *Kanal*, the film by Andrzej Wajda, wrapped in the great black cloak, which he wore deep inside and brought back from hell.

Sergio danced the "Mephisto Waltz" at the Hotel Bristol before writing it, or at the Pera Palace in Istanbul. At the Ritz in Madrid he melted like a candle in the arms of La Pasionaria and in Barcelona he embraced Marietta Karapetiz and whisked her across the dance floor in wicked and liberating waltzes, thousands of waltzes on the bank of the Rhine, the same ones that caused the venerable and magical Giuseppe di Lampedusa to twirl in Garibaldi's Italy. Czechoslovakia, Hungary, and Russia offered him the same snows, the same somnambulism. Central Asia did not take him out of himself, immersed in his illnesses and convalescences, in his long dialogues with another disappearing apparition, the writer Juan Manuel Torres, in improbable settings that latched on to his suit like misery latched on to the world.

All Sergio Pitol's characters, or almost all, wake up in the hospital, and when they don't, they lose interest in what they set out to do, which is also a kind of hospitalization. His stories are always a story within another story, memories within other memories, nothing is ever direct, one has to turn with him, or when it suits him, unravel the story, a Russian doll, a box full of surprises, a jack-in-the-box propelled by a spring, a prank that pops out, a spurt of water that soaks you, a pie in the face, a viper that bites just when the author is about to tame it.

An odd character, Sergio, the more he wrote, the more elusive and remote he became; the narrower the boundaries between the fantastic and the real, the more indispensable. Pitol felt less uprooted the farther away he was and able to be found as Margarita García Flores found him in Paris, in his apartment in the Trocadéro, a stone's throw from the Bois de Boulogne.

Later, with the Cervantes Prize painted on his smile, he

walked through the streets of Xalapa where everyone greeted him, embraced him, congratulated him, recognized him in "recognition," grateful for his having rewarded them and for remaining within reach of their Mexican—or rather Xalapeño—embrace.

His mother, Cristina Deméneghi, drowned in the Atoyac River, during an outing in the countryside. Unwittingly, his mother bequeathed to her son his status as a castaway, which never left him. Sergio Pitol was always part sea and part sailor. He always returned but only later did he remain in Mexico. To stay must have been for him a kind of death, and Mexico City a port of catastrophe, to settle down, something akin to mummification, because Pitol burned all his ships.

Ever since Sergio published his first story, his heroes and heroines always seemed eccentric because if Sergio parodies, he never provides us the key, it could be the Mock Turtle and not the novelist María Luisa Mendoza; it could be Marietta Karapetiz and not the latinist Mathilde Lemberger. Sergio Pitol is not interested in revealing anything, much less providing explanations. He throws out his book, and that's it. The rest is a matter of typography. Oh, and of Sacha, which was his dog's name and also one of the characters in his novel *Taming the Divine Heron*! Pitol was never interested in anyone who didn't write or at least love books, and Sacha, like Jan Kott, was an expert on Shakespeare.

Sergio Pitol, an aristocrat to the tip of his toes, a maker of illusions, a *bon vivant*, the owner of stables full of unicorns, a great connoisseur of painting, a lover of antique furniture, and discoverer of works of art in Poland and Istanbul; he would walk with his cane (which he didn't need but accentuated his elegance) through his properties in his native Xalapa, in the state of

Veracruz, like the Marquis de Carabas, gesturing: "Those corn-fields are mine!"

The author of the extraordinary *The Magician of Vienna*, he quickly became a native of Poland out of the great love he had for its people and its literature, and he found time to write books of short stories and novels that earned him the Cervantes Prize in 2005.

I remember his anger when he told me that "the Mexican leftists go to Moscow to find formulas that fit within their intractable creeds." It irritated him to be given classes in socialism with pre-established and punitive manuals. He told me that when he arrived in Poland—where he worked as a cultural attaché—the reality was totally different "because life is much stronger, national circumstances are different than those that appear in the socialist books we read in Mexico."

There are things that Sergio simply does not want to do, and one must accept it or throw in with him, join him secretly or underground, accept his mysterious, his special literary vibration, despite the work it demands. Even then, one becomes trapped by his language, in his writing that links reflections, and enter that gloomy bar in Warsaw, look for the horizon facing the Sopot Sea, and realize that men and women are also settings where comedies or tragedies play out. There is never dialogue in Pitol, only relationships, and it is only possible to "enjoy the beauty of certain phrases."

Sergio once gave Margarita García Flores a phrase key to understanding his work: "Usually, when I write a story, there is an area of emptiness, a kind of psychological cave that I'm not interested in filling." The characters of *Mephisto's Waltz* inhabit this space, which can be as insalubrious as the Córdoba of his childhood.

These are stories that bewitch, stories with open arms, stories that sing like a river. Flowing. Different streams converge in them in perfect harmony and Pitol, that great magician, orchestrates their waters, traces their path along the earth, deepens their bed, polishes their reflections, and sometimes plays and plunges us into laughter because it's always healthy to drown, if only for a moment, anyone who believes they can swim upstream.

ELENA PONIATOWSKA AMOR

VICTORIO FERRI TELLS A TALE

for Carlos Monsiváis

I know my name is Victorio. I know people think I'm mad (a fiction that at times infuriates me and at others merely amuses me). I know I'm different from the others, but my father, my sister, my cousin José, and even Jesusa, are different too, and no one thinks they're mad; worse things are said about them. I know we're nothing like other people, but even among us there isn't a hint of similarity. I've heard it said that my father is the devil, and though I've never seen any external mark that identifies him as such, my conviction that he is who he is remains incorruptible. Even so, at times it's a source of pride; in general, it neither pleases nor frightens me to be one of the evil one's offspring.

When a peon dares to speak about my family, he says that our house is hell itself. Before hearing that assertion the first time, I imagined the devil's abode to be different (I thought, of course, of the traditional flames), but I changed my mind and gave credence to the words when after a painful and arduous meditation it occurred to me that none of the houses I know looks like ours. Evil does not dwell in them, but it dwells in ours.

My father's wickedness is so prodigious that it exhausts me; I've seen the pleasure in his eyes when he orders a peon locked in the rooms at the back of the house. When he orders them flogged

I

and contemplates the blood that flows from their shredded backs, he bares his teeth in delight. He's the only one on the hacienda who's able to laugh this way, although I'm learning to do it too. My laugh is becoming so terrifying that women cross themselves upon hearing it. We both bare our teeth and emit a sort of gleeful bray when we're overcome with satisfaction. None of the peons dares laugh like us, not even when they're weary from drink. Joy, if they can remember it, confers on their faces a grimace that doesn't quite form a smile.

Fear has been exalted on our properties. My father has assumed his father's position, and when he in turn disappears I shall become the lord of the comarca; I shall become the devil: I'll be the Lash, the Fire, and the Punishment. I shall oblige my cousin José to accept money in exchange for his share of the hacienda, and, because he prefers life in the city, he'll be able to go to that part of Mexico he's always talking about, which only God knows whether it exists or whether he merely imagines it in order to make us jealous; and I shall keep for myself the lands, the houses, and the men, and the river where my father drowned his brother Jacobo, and, much to my woe, the sky that blankets us every day, in a different color, with clouds that change from one moment to the next, only to change again. I endeavor to look up as little as possible, such does it terrify me when things are not the same, when they escape dizzyingly from my sight. Whereas Carolina, to annoy me, despite the fact I'm her elder and she should show me respect, spends long periods of time gazing at the sky, and at night, during dinner, adorned with a silly expression that dares not come from ecstasy, remarks that the evening clouds were golden on a lilac background, or that at dusk the water's color succumbed to that of fire, and other such non-sense. If anyone in our house is truly possessed with madness, it would be she. My father, indulgent, feigns excessive attention and encourages her to continue, as if the foolishness he's hearing made any sense to him! He never speaks to me during meals, but it would be silly for me to resent it, as I am the only one he favors with his intimacy each morning, at sunrise, when I'm just getting home and he, with coffee in hand that he sips hurriedly, sets out to the fields to become drunk on the sun and violently stupefy himself with the harshest of tasks. Because the devil (I have yet to understand why, but he does) is compelled by necessity to forget his crime. If I drowned Carolina in the river, I'm certain that I wouldn't feel the slightest remorse. Perhaps one day, when I rid myself of these filthy sheets that no one has bothered to change since I fell ill, I shall do it. Then I'll be able to feel myself in my father's skin, to know firsthand what I intuit in him, even though, regrettably, incomprehensibly, a difference will forever stand between us: he loved his brother more than the palm tree he planted in front of the colonnade, and his chestnut mare and the filly she foaled; whereas to me Carolina is nothing more than an inconvenient weight and nauseating presence.

These days, illness has led me to rip away more than one veil that until now had remained untouched. Despite having always slept in this room, I can say it is only now betraying its secrets. I had never noticed, for example, that there are ten beams that span the ceiling, or that on the wall opposite where I now lie there are two large spots caused by the humidity, or that, and I find this oversight unbearable, beneath the heavy mahogany dresser dozens of mice have built nests. The desire to catch them and feel their beating death on my lips torments me. But such pleasure is, for now, forbidden me.

Do not think that the many discoveries I make day after day reconcile me to my illness, nothing of the sort! The yearning, more intense with each passing moment, for my nightly escapades is constant. Sometimes I wonder if someone is taking my place, if someone whose name I do not know is usurping my duties. That sudden concern disappears at the very moment it is born; it overjoys me to think that no one on the hacienda is able to fulfill the requirements that such a laborious and delicate occupation demands. Only I, who am known to the dogs, the horses, the domestic animals, am able to get close enough to the shanties to hear what the laborers are whispering without causing the barking, clucking, or braying that such animals would make to betray someone else.

I provided my first service without realizing it. I discovered that behind Lupe's house a mole had dug a hole. Lying there, lost in the contemplation of the hole, I spent many an hour waiting for the odd-looking creature to appear. Instead, I watched, to my regret, the sun defeated once again, and with its annihilation I was overwhelmed by a deep sleep that was impossible to resist. When I awoke, night had fallen. Inside the shanty, you could hear the soft murmur of hasty and trusting voices. I pressed my ear to a crevice, and for the first time I discovered the tales that were circulating about my house. When I repeated the conversation, my service was rewarded. It seems that my father was flattered when it was revealed to him that I, against all expectation, might be useful to him. I was happy because, from that moment, I occupied an undeniably superior position to Carolina.

Three years have passed since my father ordered Lupe to be punished for being a malcontent. The passage of time has made a man of me, and, thanks to my work, I have accumulated knowledge that, while natural to me, does not cease to be remarkable: I have managed to see into the deepest night; my ear has become as sharp as the otter's; I walk so stealthily, so, if it can be said, wingedly, that a squirrel would envy my steps; I can lie on the roofs of the shacks and remain there for long periods of time until I hear those words that my mouth will repeat later. I am able to sniff out those who are going to speak. I can say, proudly, that my nights are rarely wasted, since from the looks on their faces, from the way in which their mouths quiver, from a certain twitch that I perceive in their muscles, from an aroma that emanates from their bodies, I am able to identify those whom a final shame, or the embers of dignity, rancor, despair, will drag through the night toward confidences, confessions, whispers. I have managed to go undiscovered during these three years; and to attribute to satanic powers my father's ability to know their words and to punish them. In their guilelessness, they come to believe this to be one of the devil's qualities. I laugh. My certainty that he is the devil has much deeper roots.

Sometimes, just to amuse myself, I go and spy on Jesusa's hut. There I have been allowed to contemplate how her firm petite body becomes intertwined with my father's old age. Their lewd contortions delight me. I tell myself, deep inside, that Jesusa's tenderness should be directed at me, that I am her same age, and not at the evil one, who long ago turned seventy.

The doctor has come on several occasions. He examines me with pretentious concern. He turns to my father and in a grave and compassionate voice declares that there is no cure, that any treatment is useless, and that it is merely a question of awaiting death. At that moment, I see how my father's green eyes grow brighter. A look of glee (of mockery) comes over them, and by then I cannot contain a thunderous peal of laughter that causes the doctor to grow pale with incomprehension and fear. When he at last leaves, the sinister one also unleashes a guffaw, pats me on the back, and we both laugh like madmen.

It is known that among the many misfortunes that can beset man, the worst arise from loneliness, which, I sense, is attempting to fell me, to break me, to put thoughts into my mind. Until a month ago I was completely happy. I spent my mornings sleeping; during the afternoon, I'd wander the countryside, go to the river, or lie face down on the grass, waiting for the hours to come and go. At night, I'd listen. It was always painful for me to think; so, I avoided doing it. Now, I think of things, and that terrifies me. Even though I know I'm not going to die, that the doctor is mistaken, that there will always be a man at Refugio, because when the father dies the son must assume command: that's how it has always been, and things can't suddenly be any other way (which is why my father and I, when anyone says otherwise, burst into laughter). But when alone and sad and at the end of a long day, I begin to think, I'm overwhelmed with doubts. I have concluded that nothing inevitably happens in just one way. The repetition of the most trivial facts produces variations, exceptions, nuances. Why, then, should the hacienda not be without the son to replace the master? I have been vexed by something more unsettling of late, as I think about the possibility that my father may believe that I'm going to die and that his laughter may have been something other than mere mocking of the doctor, but rather the delight that my disappearance produces in him, the joy of finally ridding himself of my voice and my presence. It is possible that those who hate me have succeeded in convincing him of my madness ...

In the Ferri chapel in the parish church of San Rafael there is a small plaque that reads:

Victorio Ferri died in childhood.
His father and sister remember him with love.

Mexico City, 1957

LIKE THE GODS

for José Emilio Pacheco

The matron noticed that his eyes—accustomed as she was to the patient and the inexorable scrutiny of his march toward decay, she was unable to hide the wince of disgust that they invariably produced in her!—had come to rest on the dirty, yellowing page of a newspaper lifted with difficulty from the bench where he lay. His unsteady gaze seemed to linger on a scrap of paper among whose folds, smudges, and assorted wear and tear, there were noticeable signs that grasped and connected the scattered flashes of his attention, as if in some remote area of consciousness, a slight opening had appeared.

Surprised, the matron considered the possibility that inside his chalky flesh, at last, an impulse had surfaced that for three years (since that absurd and tragic night when everything that stirred within him had been fulfilled, in which his being had been satisfied to the fullest extent allowed) had been groping, muted and unsuccessful, to emerge into the light. But the impulse, if there was one, stopped without ever manifesting itself in any specific movement, defeated by the first of many obstacles that interrupted a long journey. His inability to overcome them explained how, at thirteen years of age, he found himself there, detained, confined, shattered by a fate that had driven him for as long as he possessed the use of reason and whose first manifestation had been the unbounded and abominable use of memory with which he had succeeded in making his parents and fellow believers confuse him with the Miracle Bearer. (The number of verses monotonously recited was for his mother cause for an ever-renewed astonishment.) But the root of her personal pride did not lie in the broad knowledge of Scripture he possessed, but in the host of forbidden prayers and supplications whose arduous learning his parents ignored, and in the store of resentment and restrained violence that he knew to conceal under the mask of a submissive gaze and a somewhat servile smile whose goodness it would have been deemed loathsome to doubt.

And it was not at all misguided to think that something had been shaken inside him when confronted with the blurred photograph being contemplated on a worn newspaper page, whose printed words no longer transmitted any message to him at all, but on which, captivated and absorbed, he did his best to inspect an open mouth, where teeth like grains of corn shot out and made a gesture of helplessness, and guns that pointed at the body of the woman to whom that mouth belonged, and, in addition, a small bundle held by the spent and withered arms of the woman who bore that foolish, delirious mouth, where, on display, without the slightest concern or mercy, were imploring grains of corn and a sharp, sterile tongue, paralyzed by the prospect of those black steel barrels that pointed at her and whose vomit of fire would cause her to toss the bundle wrapped in her blanket, which would surely wail as it fell with a bitter and shrill cry, only then to remain motionless, without the slightest whimper announcing its existence, awaiting a boot to crush it and the hoof of a horse driven mad by the smoke and the crackling of the fire to penetrate it only to be stained with a thick and violent cherry color that the dust would immediately turn, to the delight of the flies, into a coarse and viscous crust.

A group of loose and confused images sought out, fiercely, clumsily, stubbornly, the path that would lead them outside and only succeed in producing an imbecilic stupor, a ferocious perplexity within that amorphous mass of colorless flesh inside of which one would imagine that the bones would continue to float without order or coherence in a dense liquid (impossible to think of blood, rather a repugnant and toxic water), without their eyes being able to undermine something other than their usual idiocy; full of incomprehension and fear before that world of violent and quivering mouths that from time to time, before an external stimulus, of which she caught a fleeting glimpse of people scattered in all directions, of horses' hooves to which blood, the flesh and blood of their brothers and sisters, would stick to provide that reddish color that would torment him obsessively in the days that followed the disaster. (The world began to take on a crimson color, and the desolation, the horror, and the shrill cries that preceded that night were accompanied always by the most frantic purple hues.) When he had still not attempted it in his present dwelling, a small thatch hut where he was cared for by a dirty old woman who cried each time she passed her coarse, gaunt hand through his hair, insisting in her invitation to sleep, to eat, even to be understood, only then he was beginning not to understand, to lose himself in an deeply intricate maze in which he was learning to live at the same time the role of a fly and a spider; without even being able to transmit the urgency of a consolation which the old woman's tears and caresses could not lend him, but which had to come from the Word itself, transferred and reflected by Him to the awareness of some of his servants, although it would be necessary for them to repeat each sentence to him a thousand times (while at one time, a then that was barely an immediate past or a present that had not completely disappeared, he had known by heart more psalms than any other member of the community, as well as the endless prayers of the creed which was neither his or his parents', but of those who had managed to expel him from schools, of the mothers of his classmates who with muddled words threw him out of their houses, and of the men and women who, one night in October, driven by madness, the heat, the urgency to impose on the ground—where they trampled a law and a punishment that was closer to their convictions and protected what they considered their rights—and possibly by a good dose of aguardiente, had given way to their passions, uniting themselves to him and his unlimited rancor in order to proceed so that the small group that poisoned the air of San Rafael with their songs of doom and their humble pride would atone for their sins). He, who possessed a prodigious memory, he, who knew how to conceive the most subtle robes with which to boast of humiliation and perfidy, realized that the simplest of information was rapidly getting away from him, that something in him was refusing to retain the elements that reality offered him, and before entering that total night that he felt was destined and supposed near, he needed the caress, not the one that the mime of the hands gave him that were curtailed in the hair, but one that had to come from the voice, a voice that someone (anyone) emitted and managed to persuade him (the night advanced with a quickness that he could not, or he did not want, or simply did not care, to diminish) that the only guilty person—and because He could not be called guilty—was the Lord. But the lightning bolt of grace of the redeeming word never appeared, except in his own mouth, muttering inwardly, barely moving his lips, acting and listening at the same time so that, if the mistake occurred, only he would notice it, for not even then did pride abandon him, and he would not have been forgiven—although forgiveness and pride and ultimately the same prevailing pride could, under such circumstances, before the spilt blood and the wailing of his people, and the wrath that his action would unleash, and the violent ashes of walls because of the rancor of the One who is forever and ever on high, seem puerile—no mistake that would defile, in the eyes of the others, his reputation as a precocious genius.

So, he preferred not to speak, to maintain that silence, alert and awaiting the furtive message that would grant him redemption and forgiveness.

Perhaps it was the desperation of lying in wait that postponed his agony and delayed his entrance into the world of shadows, in which now, almost inert, he lay, cowlike, against the loose images that a newspaper tossed about and which fought to be introduced and provide him with the thread with which to tie together blurred memories of which, in the same way that he had forgotten what effect was due to what cause, which moment was the fatal and unavoidable result of another, he could not distinguish whether they should produce joy or fear in him. Even as they picked his body up from the middle of the street that cursed midnight in which, driven by a frenzy that flashed through the pit of his stomach, his heart, his brain, all throughout him, he shouted insults at his family and cried out to the others and urged them to spill blood until the crimes committed against the faith had been completely washed away, until purification was achieved, he could no longer reconstruct the facts completely; when the strong arms of a man came to rescue him, from the blood and the ashes and the flames through which he believed he had distinguished the tremendous gaze of his mother, and handed him over to other arms, which deposited him in others, who in turn transferred the mission to others, only to interrupt at last the chain in a miserable shack on the shores of San Rafael, where a dirty and sad woman, as dirty as the planks of her ramshackle hut, whose sadness likened her to her arid parcel of land, ran a hand through his hair, while her dry, sunken eyes stared at him without love, and her voice, instead of issuing a pardon, urged him to tasks of no moral content, such as eating, sleeping, trying to cut the subtle threads of memory, as if it were so simple, that one only needed to propose it so that a lifetime, whole years with their months, their weeks, their days and their hours devoted to praise and to the attainment of an idea which he fixedly obeyed, were totally and definitely erased! For it was not only an act, that of denunciation, which necessarily had to be forgotten in order to be at peace with oneself (a moment which in itself would appear to be monstrous to people because it did not relate to the absolute idea of the Glory of God, before which all human smallness became insignificant, banal), but an infinite and complex set of moments married to each other, which arose from the very moment in which his conscience was born, since the germ dwelled in him from the beginning, since they tried to introduce him to the elements of faith, and enlightened placed in doubt, and now forever, not only his greatness but also his truthfulness. Thus, when, later on, it was time to attend school, his companions began to single him out and make him the victim of such an unimaginable variety of insults that the principal himself, who had come to consider him the source of the unruliness, refused to allow him to come to school; he did not hold grudges against them, since on the contrary any other conciliatory or fraternal attitude would have seemed repugnantly tepid to him; and then, when the word persecution was applied to others (to those who were then the active subjects of every relationship in which such a term came into play) it acquired a palpable and unequivocal meaning, and those who had previously repudiated him dreaded the fear of the humiliation of being watched, and the temples offered for worship were converted into barracks or simply closed, and the most holy hearts of Jesus withdrew, banished, to their hiding places, and some grotesque dolls were dressed in cassocks and chasubles to exhibit them shamelessly to public taunts, and scorn clung to churches and sanctuaries, and the old women shrieked in the squares and markets, and his father's activities grew untimely, and his visits to celebrate service in the neighboring villages, Peñuela, Amatlán, Coscomatepec, San Rafael, with the complicity of the authorities and the stalking eyes of the faithful of the persecuted worship, and the prison and the firing squad were the daily ration of pain and sacrifice for a clergy whom he saw as too submissive, and before him and his presumed candor his most bitter glances fell, and he was spat upon and vexed for being an enemy of God, when indeed he was His instrument, his form of punishment, his flaming sword, the angel, bearer of vengeance, he felt a desire to confess his love, poured out during so many years of clandestine storage, by the creed in disgrace, but the feeling that it would have been to act with wild precipitation stopped him just in time; he had to maintain the masquerade until the appointed moment had come; certain, confident in emerging invictus over the fear or remorse that such an action might cause him, since he did not recount then about his conscience the crushing sickness that doubt causes; and it was for this reason that he was no longer sure of the goodness of an act whose consummation he had caused, he demanded (without anyone responding to his ardent supplication), even if it were only in murmurs, the redeeming word. Wreathed in the fire of his doubt, gripped by the embers that consumed him until his entrance into the darkness, where gradually fear, doubt, colors, images became diluted, erased, until allowing the escape of the sinister memory of that time of exaltation and anger in which one afternoon, with entrails aflame and urine paralyzed in his kidneys, he wrote with his firm handwriting of a diligent pupil, to the people whom it concerned, some lines where he stated that it had been his family who reported to the authorities the hiding place of Father Crespo (whom, as soon as he was captured, they had hung from a tree in the poplar grove), and the next day the house was selected with great care and the religious service had to be done in even greater secrecy than ever because his father felt that the climate was conducive to disorder and he could verify that his letter had taken effect, and they appeared in the mouth and in the conscience of all as the victimizers of the hanged priest. Later, when he was still able, he remembered that he had heard voices in the street that night, demanding that the house of Serafín Naranjo be set afire where his father was holding the service, and some had arrived with rifles, others with torches, and others with stones, and others with nothing, with only a ranting mouth and strong fists, determined that no one should leave the house, while he, with a voice made powerful by passion and that stood out from the general roar, cried for justice for the murdered priests, of whose martyrdom, he swore, were responsible those twenty people gathered to intone chants and prayers in a low voice. And then everything became fire, which passed from torches to walls and turned men's eyes into a coppery mirror of the fire, and three blond men wearing heavy boots fired their rifles at the doors when the faithful tried to escape from the smoke and the flames, and the crowd grew and hatred grew louder, stronger, spreading fraternally from one hand to another, from one mouth to another, and a woman, perhaps Ignacia, desperately tried to leave with a small bundle that was crying in her hands, and a shot rang out and the bundle fell, and then one of the three blond men while running crushed it, and a horse suddenly had a red hoof, while he, from the sidewalk, kneeling down, on the hard paving stones, immutable before the roar that surrounded him, asked that the Lord strengthen the punishment of the wicked, pleaded for the fire to engulf them, when his mother's face emerged from a burning window, and a stone struck her forehead, and, terrified, her gaze fixed on the one who, exalted, accepted with profound unction the agony of the sinners, the purification of the people. He witnessed still the collapse of the ceilings and felt the burning ash on his face and breathed in with horrified delight the smell that the heap of smoldering rubble and charred bodies gave off, and could no longer see anything because a man snatched him from his

17

delirium, and after moving through numerous sets of hands, rough and strange, he was deposited in the hut of a foolish old woman, where his communication with the Lord was completely interrupted, and from there they had led him to that building where on one of its benches he now lay, gazing enraptured at the blurred photograph of an old newspaper, without even knowing why, furiously striking the matron every time she tried to take it away, immersed in a total nothingness into which he stubbornly tried to incorporate that mouth that she saw confronting a rifle.

Mexico, 1958

THE PANTHER

for Elena Poniatowska

None of the magics that traversed my childhood can compare to his apparition. Nothing I've conceived so far has succeeded in blending refinement with ferocity so superbly. During the ensuing nights, I implored his presence, amused at first, but ultimately impatient and on the verge tears. My mother used to say that one day I'd end up dreaming about bandits from having played at them so often. And, indeed, by the end of vacation, persecution and infamy, rage and blood haunted my nights. During that time, going to the movies meant enjoying a single feature with slight variations from one showing to the next: the unchanging subject was provided courtesy of the Allied offensive against the Axis armies. A single afternoon with a triple feature (during which we watched with unspeakable delight mortars rain down on a phantasmagoric Berlin where buildings, vehicles, temples, faces, and palaces dissolved into a single immense lake of fire; epic pledges of love, a penumbra of air raid shelters in a London of broken obelisks and large buildings without façades, and Veronica Lake's tresses impassively resisting Japanese shrapnel while a group of wounded soldiers was being evacuated from a rocky islet in the Pacific) was enough to cause the roar of bullets to pierce my room that night while a multitude of mangled bodies and the skulls of nurses propelled my startled self to seek refuge in the room of my older brothers.

Fully aware of the risks, I invented contrived games that no one found amusing. I replaced the customary antagonism between cops and robbers, consecrated by custom and fashion, or the new one, between the Allies and the Germans, with other savage and extravagant protagonists. Games in which panthers launched a surprise attack against a village, frantic hunts in which panthers howled in pain and fury after being snared by ruthless hunters, bloody fights between panthers and cannibals. But neither they nor the frequency with which I read adventure books in the jungle made the repetition of the vision possible.

His image persisted for what seemed like a long period of time. I carelessly set out to prove that the figure was becoming increasingly weaker, his features gently blurred. The trampled flow of forgetfulness and recollections that is time destroys the will to secure a feeling forever in our memory. At times, I felt an urgent need to hear the message that my half-wittedness had prevented him from delivering the night of his apparition. This enormous and beautiful animal whose shiny blackness rivaled the night traced an elegant course around the room; he walked toward me, opened his jaws and, seeing the terror that gripped me, closed them, offended. He left in the same nebulous way in which he had appeared. For days I blamed myself for my lack of courage. I cursed myself for daring to imagine that this gorgeous beast wanted to devour me. His expression was friendly, supplicant; his snout seemed more eager for play and petting than for the aftertaste of blood.

New hours quickly took the place of old ones. New dreams

eliminated the one that for so long had been my constant passion. The panther games not only came to seem foolish, but also incomprehensible, as I could no longer remember with precision how they began. I was able to return to my lessons, to buckle down and practice my handwriting and the passionate handling of colors and lines.

Twenty trivial, happy, profane, intense, hazy, awkwardly hopeful, broken, deceptive, and dark years had to pass in order for last night to arrive, when, to my surprise, as if in the middle of that barbarous childhood dream, I heard once again an animal pant as it penetrated the adjoining room. The irrational that courses through our being at times adopts a gallop so frenzied that we cravenly seek refuge in that stale set of rules with which we aim to regulate existence, those vacuous canons with which we attempt to halt the flight of our deepest instincts. So, even in sleep, I tried to appeal to rational explanations: I argued that the noise was caused by a cat going into the kitchen to polish off the table scraps. Comforted by this explanation, I dreamt that I fell back asleep only to reawaken soon after, sensing, with absolute clarity, his presence next to me. There he was, opposite the bed, contemplating me with an expression of delight. In my dream, I was able to recall the previous vision. The intervening years had only succeeded in modifying the setting. The heavy dark wood furniture was gone, as was the oil lamp that hung over my bed; the walls were different, only my expectations and the panther remained the same: as if only a few brief seconds had passed between the two nights. Joy, mixed with a hint of fear, coursed through me. I recalled in minute detail the first visit; attentive and astonished, I awaited his message.

Haste did not grip the animal. He paced before me languidly, tracing small circles; then, in a single pounce he reached the fireplace, stirred the ashes with his forepaws, and returned to the center of the room; he stared at me, opened his jaws, and finally decided to speak.

Anything I might say about the happiness I felt at the time would only impoverish it. My destiny revealed itself in the clearest possible way in the words of that ebony divinity. My feeling of elation reached an unbearable degree of perfection. It was beyond comparison. Nothing—not even one of those few ephemeral moments in which we glimpse eternity upon discovering true happiness—has ever produced in me the effect achieved by his message.

The excitement awakened me, but the vision disappeared; nonetheless, those prophetic words, which I scribbled down immediately on a piece of paper that I found on the desk, remained alive, as if etched in iron. As I returned to bed, half-asleep, I couldn't help but know that an enigma had been solved, the true enigma, and that the obstacles that had reduced my days to a single horizonless time fell vanquished.

The alarm clock rang. I looked with delight at the page on which those twelve enlightening words were inscribed. Leaping to read them would have been the easiest course of action, but such immediacy would not have been in keeping with the solemnity of the occasion. Rather than yielding to that desire, I headed to the bathroom; I dressed myself slowly, carefully, with a forced parsimony; I drank a cup of coffee, after which, trembling and slightly shaken, I rushed to read the message.

Twenty years passed before the panther returned. The amazement he engendered in me on both occasions cannot have been gratuitous. The paraphernalia with which the dream was marked cannot be attributed to mere coincidence. No; something in his eyes, above all in his voice, seemed to suggest that he was not the mere image of an animal, but rather the possibility of communing with a force and an intelligence that were beyond the mere human. And, yet, I must confess that the words I had scribbled down were nothing more than an enumeration of trivial and anodyne nouns that made no sense. For a moment I doubted my sanity. I reread them carefully, rearranged them as if I were trying to piece together a puzzle. I combined all the words into a single, long word; I studied each syllable. I spent days and nights in minute and sterile philological combinations. I succeeded in clarifying nothing. Scarcely the knowledge that the hidden signs have been consumed by the same foolishness, the same chaos, the same inconsistency from which quotidian events suffer.

I trust, however, that, someday, the panther will return.

Mexico City, May 1960

BODY PRESENT

for Neus Espresate

At the moment when the senselessness of the world was revealed to Daniel Guarneros, his conscience fell into undeniable contradictions; he discovered the taste of violent, extreme rancor which, once laid bare, left him as surprised as if he harbored a fire within himself, which he had only been able to notice when it had already overcome the foundations, when every possible act—whether the chosen path were this one or that—would be nothing but a collapse, a collection of ash and rubble, of baffling and useless specks. Why so suddenly? he wondered, dismayed before the bottle of brandy that, without the possibility of despair, already stunned, he slowly consumed in one of the many bars that populated the city. He had felt sick many times, ill at ease with his circumstances, weary from the cronyism, the petty ploys that had served him to reach the position he currently enjoyed, but those were desperate times—and therein lay the essential distinction—that could be erased, destroyed with cognac, whiskey, or tequila. What happened today was entirely different. The attack grew colder, more overwhelming: an unexpected glance at his naked gut before a mirror, a forced look, the truth, inward, and alcohol had no effect or power to soothe the terrains of his conscience that had turned into an open sore. He had drunk more than three-quarters of the bottle without managing to recover, that is to get drunk, forget, reaching, at most, a certain confusion of dates and events, of courtesies and betrayals, phrases and facts taken from the wide-ranging reserve contained in his memory. Somewhere within us—he seemed to hear—everything, always, is here and now. What is past does not flow, it stagnates, it stops and becomes fixed with extremely clear profiles, and at the precise moment (that instant whose election has nothing to do with will or desire) arises to save or condemn the person inside of whom it resides. Fearful of the revelations it sensed, it attempted to unseat, to tarnish memories. So, for example, he could not— and this imprecision made him happy—remember if the statement, "you're evil; from now on you'll be more and more so. The Daniel I loved is gone forever," had come to his mind as *the moment it all happened,* and he discovered his helplessness or thereafter, sitting in front of the bottle, when trying to forget the trance, to his misfortune, made it closer and more tangible.

He must consider, he told himself at first without managing to convince himself, the fatigue: in recent months his business had required too much attention, and this trip was not as restful as those of previous years. Having included Juan Felipe in the program gave it a different character. It meant, by necessity, adding too many activities, doing too many things that diminished the tranquility, the appeal of diversion. They descended to the status of American tourists in an incessant and pointless waddle from one place to another. None other than yesterday, while walking along the paths of Villa Adriana, which because it was so devastated could contribute little to anyone who like he frequented for some time the authentic sources of art and of history, or in former days, when touring the museums and Roman galleries (which during previous visits they had rejected, since for them it was a waste of time to go to those places they knew almost by heart, forgotten because they are so well known) he grew so utterly bored. Everything had become a nightmare since the day of arrival itself, when the dandy had the idea of burying his nose in guidebooks and maps to discover that there was this museum, the other, that gallery, the church of Santa So-and-so, the monument X, Y, and Z, who regularly, accompanied by his mother, devoted his time to knowing, to obeying to the letter the recommendations that the stupid books dictated. If one could only have seen the poor yokel dazzled by the novelty of everything old!, Antoinette herself, whose childhood had been spent in a pleasant Parisian exile, who had used her first honeymoon to discover the Orient and year after year spent autumn in Europe by his side, with what foolish air, of a giddy little girl, waited for him at lunchtime:

"Today we walked from the Piazza Venezia to San Giovanni in Laterano, can you imagine? Tomorrow's itinerary includes a trip to Villa Borghese, so Juan Felipe can see the sculpture of Paolina."

And he—who always resented the excessive presence of his wife and maintained that a man should be able to live it up freely without a carping and solicitous wife by his side, in those first days in Rome, alone, free—began to feel the need, then the urgency, to be among family. I grow old, he had thought a few evenings after his arrival, when in the bar at the Excelsior, instead of responding to the obvious lure of a fabulous blonde, he meditated on the insipid days that Antonieta and her stepson were forcing upon him: getting out of a taxi to take photographs, getting back into the car that would take them to the next site recommended in the guidebook, until, almost inadvertently, he decided he would join them and share their trips and arrive finally to that awful Saturday in September where from the always invariable Piazza Venezia they had initiated a tour of the Corso only to end up at the church of Santa Maria del Popolo, and there, as he contemplated a fresco—perhaps the first mural he had seen in Rome about thirty years before—he turned his face, looked at his wife, and could no longer restrain a tidal wave of disgust that included Juan Felipe, the few tourists, and the faithful who at that hour were roaming the temple and returned to it like a macabre boomerang. He knew at that moment how much he detested himself and to what extent the facts that made up his life had become stupid and ignoble. Any words would have been trivial; he fled the church and walked for hours through a Rome that autumn's dusk magnified; pine trees of purple and gold against a thick black backdrop revealed in an equivocal and complex way the passionate, lustful, and delirious character of the city. Defeated by fatigue, he entered a bar to drink and semi-remember and in that semi-remembering to invade the very origin of his current distress, only to reach a state where he no longer knew whether it was due to alcohol or to a variety of situations: fortune, jobs, women, his comings and goings, as if he were handling a deck of ID cards belonging to different individuals, which, as if by magic, suffered from the same legal personality. The names alike, the last names identical.

The boy Daniel Guarneros who played ball with a group of friends in the extremely long, desolate streets of the colonia San

Rafael, while waiting for his mother who sewed buttons in a small shirt factory; Daniel Guarneros and his mother, that night when they walked almost racing amid frightened and equally hasty people, because that night the Villistas would enter the city and there was talk about the possibility of bloody, harum-scarum fighting—God only knows!—in the streets. Daniel Guarneros, present!, at the Melchor Ocampo school, and the first nighttime outings to see Italian films at the Rialto and to dance randy dan-zones at El Apache.

"When a man finds an old woman he's ruined," he told him-self stupidly, while the blonde he'd seen the evening before at the bar in the Excelsior smiled at him, slowly sipping, with a kind of affected disinterest, the contents of her glass. "Did I sleep with her?" If he wasn't even sure whether three or four days ago he had, how could one suppose that those ancient and dusty memo-ries that he so infrequently summoned, were, in fact, real, that he was not confusing them, making them up?

"Look, darlin'," he heard himself say a while later, when there was already a new bottle and she was beside him, "even if you spoke my language, you wouldn't be able to understand me. How could you! We were little squirts, and the teacher had us totally convinced. The old man was a mean ol' fart, sweetheart, hey see how that even rhymed? There's not been another generation like ours in Mexico. We were willing to lay down our life, if it was necessary. We lacked a clear objective, but even so, believe you me, we spoke up in the markets, at the University, on the street where, wherever we could. A lot ended up in jail, what did it matter! We wanted to change everything. You don't under-stand! Then the SOB, he was really crafty, left Mexico and left us stranded. Some became communists then. Yep, blondie, that's right. Of course, they resisted. A man isn't born to accept dogma. Eloísa Martínez was there. Look, blondie, what you need to do is get me out of here and show me your skills. Don't worry about the check. Eloisa Martinez was always walking around talking nonsense. She was a kook, you know? A crack-brained simpleton who did everything possible to make bold statements. The only thing she loved were big words; she never even learned what we were fighting for. Everything boiled down to a blind cult of words, and the man, or whoever was speaking them. The voice and his spokesmen! She never bothered to scratch the surface a bit to see what was underneath. Her first devotion was to Vasconcelos, whose shade she followed with slavish mimicry. Deep down, she was nothing but a bitch, I'm here to tell you. Only God knows what kind of sonuvabitch she's messed up with now! One day she told me, not then, because I didn't know her that well, not even in Paris when I married her, or here where, go ahead and laugh, laugh at my expense, I came here to spend my honeymoon. See what I mean? My honeymoon with Eloísa Martínez!, and I was the evil one, and would always be. But that was later, when I accepted that position, and yet, you think I'm gonna give a damn what she says!, she can't complain about my behavior; I've been a gentleman, sweetie; I never passed along any information that could compromise her. It was my first big job, you know why I had to accept it?, that's practically where my career began, because what happened before, if you really think about it, was just something to fight about, necessary steps to be who I was, I mean, at the same time, that kind of job was another rung I had to climb to get to what I am now."

Daniel Guarneros discovered after he returned from the restroom that the blonde was gone. He would see her again. And why not! Because it was rare that anyone lost track of him. It just so happened that in those days, that day to be exact, he was fed up with the imbroglios, with the sack, with women. The ones he had enjoyed in those days! An entire collection of "little ladies of the national cinema." A gift, a trinket, a letter of introduction for So-and-so, and he had them at his disposal. Then, when he married Antonieta, he became more discreet; she was a Diaz de Landa, old aristocracy, my dear!, not some Doña Nobody, not some trashy María like the one who had blurted out that he would always be evil, *because the Daniel I loved has disappeared forever*, out of sheer decency he hadn't broken her face, or informed on her (if one could speak in terms of informing) in the report he had prepared on activities that had begun to be considered subversive; a connection that he could make better than anyone since he had firsthand information about her collaboration with others: committees in support of the expropriation of oil, groups in solidarity with the Spanish Republic, organizations against fascism, and she, Eloísa, had she not been a member of the International Red Aid, the Committee for Aid to Russia during Times of War, and other odds and ends like that? No, no, it should be made clear a thousand times that this was not a matter of betrayal. However, how difficult were for him those intersected nights of cold sweat, stifling anxiety, permeated with palpitations and unclean terrors. "Water that doesn't flow becomes stagnant," he repeated to himself, and he was one of those sensible men who moved on, matured, constantly exposed his ideas to the most merciless scrutiny. Was there a change? Well, yes, yes there was; he evolved, he was transformed, but he knew his individual destiny flowed along the stream of history. The times were different: there lay the crux of the matter Eloísa and her vagabonds, scatterbrained comrades, refused to understand; the times were not at all the same; Mexico had to industrialize, advance, develop, create capital. It was necessary in the short term to shape a structure; then, perhaps, one could move on, transform the current order of things, think about improvements, social change. He was convinced. So he accepted the post in the presidency that his friend so aptly offered him, one Deputy Guerrero.

"You've had a lot of setbacks, old man," he said after a long and imprecise circumlocution, "and don't give me any excuses, it's time you started to settle down. You'll find me in agreement with all your ideas, who wouldn't be?, believe me, the president most of all, but we can't forget the geographical situation, and the dialectics, bro, the dialectics will always be there. Notice how even the maestro approves of our line. We went too far in the past, we must recognize it honestly, and you have to admit that I'm right when I say it all ended in words, words and demagoguery, and when it came to facts, *rien*, like the French say, *rien de rien, mon cher.*"

"As if I didn't know!" he replied mechanically; "right now we must act above all partisanship ..."

"Of course, of course! You can take for granted that you're working for us now. You'll receive the appointment in a few days. Write down on this card your education and the positions you've held; later, we'll explain to you what your job will be."

It seemed that all of that was happening to someone else, to someone dreamt up, or better yet someone portended, not the person writing, amused, enthusiastic at the prospect of a lucrative salary, a house on the beach in Acapulco, broads, trips, on a greasy card in whose left corner appeared the national seal, his name, and beneath the obligatory colon:

Juris Doctorate from the Universidad Nacional,

Certificate in Economics from the Collège de France,

Consultant in such-and-such department in the Ministry
    of Finance

Consultant at the Banco Nacional de Crédito Ejidal.

"Very good. I'll give it to the ministry tomorrow," and he considered the matter closed.

It was all like a dream; as were the following days that were filled with breakfasts for key people, with a hectic grind amid handshakes, office visits, smiles of commitment, preparations for a new way of life: tailor, shops, bills; but the dream faded the first day of work, when after Marcelino Guerrero introduced him to his colleagues, his employees, his secretary, as soon as he took the snazzy, spectacular, cinematic desk, he was informed that that very afternoon a meeting was to be held to outline the campaign plan to follow, and then the nightmare began, yes, indeed very concretely, very close at hand, and the man he was, disloyal, opportunistic—careerist—loafer, the tepid fellow traveler disappeared entirely only to reveal another who deserved different adjectives: those that a language coins, for example, to describe the hyena. Hard days that, recalled through the alcohol, still produced in him a harsh disgust! But the heroic, what no one understood, and which made his conduct even more laudable, is that in such a place he discovered the value of the principles (until then, because of his dealings with his former colleagues, they had seemed like mere boasting to him). It was they he was to rely on to carry out the arduous task of restructuring that was proposed. Convinced that the country needed a favorable peace, a climate of absolute tranquility for the proper development of investment policy, he was relentless. He worked, and with him his entire body of researchers and technicians, tenaciously and mercilessly to develop that relationship on certain political activities and thus in the making of applicable means of control at the required time. He had to begin to dispel fictions, leave a clear record that there would no longer be room for disorder. The procedures that at the beginning earned him nights of unsettled sleeplessness ended up being habitual in his daily life, but that didn't stop him from thinking of retiring; what's more, he was able to admit it now that all clarifications were allowed: but also out of a fear that the situation could change (although the signs that might signal the slightest crack in that perfect order in whose creation he participated appeared nowhere) and he might be implicated, seated on the very bench where he had others sit, as soon as he concluded the mission entrusted to him. The salary was high, and from the allocated budget, which was more substantial than initially proposed, he could go pinch something with which to start investing. Where the high command was concerned, it was never missed.

"Cameriere! Eh, cameriere!"

The service was bad, slow. He wasn't in the mood to wait.

"Cameriere, what about the bill?"

He paid and stumbled off again to find the restroom. He felt like vomiting.

"Where are you, Eloísa Martínez? Look at me, drunk, dead drunk, with a wife and a stepson I don't give a shit about, still not old, with a good business, money, possibilities, and going to the dogs, Eloísa Martínez."

He toddled out to the street; later, the world was transformed into people walking with exasperating slowness, poorly lit alleyways, a doorway with a neon sign that illuminated pictures of black trumpeters, conversations in French, "that was indeed a decent language," a group of elegant and shameless youths who guffawed while strutting unrestrained under the effects of a bad orchestra, a brunette with almond-like black eyes, with a glow and reflexes that were undoubtedly produced by coke and, even later, a walk here and there, running around in the ruins of a once powerful and grand English car, pawing the thighs of the young girl with almond eyes, with the glare of cocaine, while the others huddled together, laughed wildly, uncontrollably, implacably, without respect or compassion, because, why deny it?, what man wants—a man who at twenty didn't have an English car or women with insatiable eyes and thighs to paw like these youngsters who were racing the car through hot streets, plagued with ruins, swelter, and cats, where the moon like a crucible of ice bathed everything with a surreal, drunken, fragmented light— was compassion. And he couldn't even find the word in French to express that need, not even … not even … not even … because love, because pain, because life requires compassion and he couldn't express that and, deep inside, not even believe it, because he had begun at the bottom, and he never received it or gave it; from the bottom, yes, with a mother who sewed buttons on shirts. "I've worked for you, mother, believe me. Honestly, everything

I've done has been so you could have a better life. It's not my fault that you kicked the bucket, dammit, have some decency at least, Guarneros!, that you died just when I was beginning to make things better for you."

She knitted me a sweater, you know, when I came to Paris on scholarship. She didn't want to believe it, not even to get used to the idea that things were beginning to improve for me. At the time it wasn't as easy to travel as it is today. Studying in Paris thirty years ago was indeed a feat. The poor woman thought that it wasn't going to do me any good. If she could see me now!

How magnificent was Paris in the thirties! He ran into her again there, they defined their friendship there, because to tell the truth in Mexico they barely knew each other. Of course, during the Vasconcelista campaign they were together a lot, they attended the same meetings, visited the same markets and unions, distributing propaganda, but they didn't know anything about each other's existences. Together they went to Cuernavaca and Toluca, sitting side by side; they exchanged ideas about the procedures to be adopted in the campaign, but, to his misfortune, it began to get serious in Paris the night he ran into her in a café in Saint-Michel. He had barely arrived and was feeling lost, anxious, like a yokel: she, however, was already like a fish in water, with the ridiculous airs of a bluestocking which, even if they dazzled him at the time, would now truly make him sick to his stomach. Deep down, those were beautiful days. They enjoyed themselves, talked from morning to night, visited museums, organized Sunday outings; she introduced him to her friends. No, he didn't regret having lived those times. Every now and then, amid bouts of nostalgia, they felt the vexing call of Anáhuac. They would return to create a decent, breathing life. They were all companions. They believed in Americanism as a solution. Ignacio would return to Chile, Gustavo to Bogotá. Living, for the first, for the only time, was a pleasure. Damn if it wasn't! In the meantime, they got married. He wanted to go on honeymoon to Lisbon, she to Bruges; in the end, they opted for Italy. A South American writer would take them in her car.

But the heat, but that blind, inhuman journey, in which bodies became ensnared into a single, obscene knot like a feast of spiders that sucked the life from a trapped insect, his mouth dripping breath and saliva on the back of the brunette with coke eyes, did not allow memories to flow. Instead, he distorted and confused them: his mother's face, Eloísa's thin, firm hips, the nape of the brunette's neck, the thunderous laughter of youth in the front seat, the voice of Lieutenant Colonel Hernández, the halls of the presidency, the talks with the South American poetess, the idiocy reflected in his stepson's eyes, money, and more and more elements that secretly conspired to form a face. What a small thing is man! Nothing, at the end of the day. A succession of gestures and phrases. A small thing! When he thinks he has arrived, reached the place to which he aspired for so many years and for which he fought so many battles, it's only to realize that it wasn't worth it; that no matter what he does there is something that remains forever broken, a small piece of life lost in God knows what twists and turns, and where perhaps the key lay, the watchword that would deliver one from being a rogue. No, he would have to clarify it a thousand and one times, to explain it, to repeat it thunderously to whomever refused to understand it: it was not that he felt a bit regretful at some point for having done this or that, for having associated himself with the truly dishonest, for having acquired the concession to exploit timber in the dense forests of Chiapas and southern Tabasco without scorning methods that were very close to blackmail. The research service that was available to him had allowed him to look out so many windows that in the beginning he felt vertigo, terrified of knowing certain secrets, of having the key and being able to penetrate the immense private miasma that the stakeholders maintained with such hidden rigor; then his innate caution, his sagacity, enabled him to draw on that complex network of news, and he went about acquiring, by pressing only slightly, wisely, a key to that infinite machinery, all the help and protection he needed, until they finally told him that he had been awarded the concession. And it was then that he began to tear up papers, to close drawers, to send farewell baskets of flowers and expensive perfumes and to spend several hours in the training of an ambitious young man, confident and determined like him, eager to carve out a future, and to settle for playing only the role of businessman: distinguished wife, residence in the Pedregal, January in Acapulco, autumn in Europe. Not bad! No, he couldn't regret that; he had fought with the weapons he had on hand to make a position for himself, with weapons acceptable among those who achieve it, and yet, without being able to explain why, deep down, he was nothing more than a crook, unless he takes care not to allow the possibility of that breach, to present the fragments of his life that contain all the secrets from escaping. But what good would it do to reflect, to try to find the solution, to go back to the past to demand clarifications? No amount of effort was worth it.

"Life, as they say where I come from, is a sweet potato," he declared. "Life is a sweet potato, you hear me?" he repeated softly and in a cowed tone. But he sensed that nobody was interested in his words; he was crying out to a universal and deaf ear because the brunette with the almond eyes, the young men, the frantic pace, the thickness of the air, the gasping, the unrestrained laughter were also the past, they no longer existed, and he had entered a night without echoes, a caliginous darkness, only to find himself in a salon, all brocades, glassware, and mirrors illuminated by a dim green light. Before him, distant, through a large window, the city stretched out beneath the dawn. They had thrown him on a divan as if he were a bundle, a crooked bundle, a snitch bundle, a blackmailer, a trafficker, like a bundle without a mother, while the others, lying on the floor, their eyes covered, cloistered in opaque urns of smoke, with the languor of dawn, without the least bit of passion, were speaking in monotone. He didn't understand if they were reciting a lesson or if they were playing a game that to him was unknown, mysterious, hidden, unable to locate or discover its mechanism. Did the brunette with the bright eyes have the floor, or did the old man with a sharp beard, or the fat pederast who stroked the hair of his companion with his limp hand, or did he, or she, or the one over there, or the slovenly old woman with a dingy face who, like him, sprawled on another divan, absorbed in her drunkenness? Everyone seemed to speak with one voice and, yet, he perceived their voices indistinctly, one by one:

"Piero de Benedetto de Franceschi, detto Piero della Francesca."

"Paolo Caliari, detto il Veronese."

"Jacopo Robusti, detto il Tintoretto."

"Direction? First prize? Fritz Lang?"

39

"Antonio Allegri, detto il Correggio."

"Franceso Mazzola, detto il Parmigianino,"

"Hai detto Malcolm Lowry? Quello de *Under the Volcano*?"

"Stefano di Giovanni, detto il Sassetta."

"Stendhal again, Parma; the beleaguered charterhouse."

"Bernardino Di Betto, detto il Pinturicchio."

He would have liked to get up, to crawl if necessary and participate in the absurd game, to overwhelm them with his knowledge, to shout that he had visited all the major museums of Europe, to list the gala premières that he had attended in Paris, in London, in Milan, to make *en passant* a reference to his collection of paintings, the pleasure with which Antonieta and he socialized with painters, thinkers, poets. "The poets of the diplomatic corps," he tried to mutter, "are our favorite, because they combine with talent the standards of a good... upbringing."

"Il Pinturicchio, il Pinturicchio."

"If you observe, you will see that Il Pinturicchio adds to the Renaissance painters a peculiar sense of landscape. He's Gothic out of its time."

What did the South American writer know of Renaissance painter Il Pinturicchio and of his delicate recreation of the landscape? However, they were there for the pleasure of speaking. It excited them to jump into the conversation at the slightest pretext.

"In his country," he added, "the landscape has the same quality of magic, of an image caught in the deepness of sleep. The first time, and all subsequent times I've been there, that union of vigor and poetry has dazzled me."

And she, Eloísa Martínez, interrupted in a vibrant voice:

"The last I saw of Mexico, a few hours after having left Tampico, was a horizon of mountains. A faraway line, where the peaks looked clearly, sharply drawn, and yet there was something so unreal in that presence that one had the feeling of seeing a theater curtain. You've been able to witness it, those mountains have, as the Yucatecan song says, the taste of dreaming. A German waiter, barely a boy, discovered my excitement and told me that it was the last I'd see of Mexico, a few minutes later the ship would leave the coast. I barely held back the tears. The defeat has just taken place. It came in the footsteps of the maestro. He swore at that last glimpse of his country that he would return only to cleanse it, to fight against those who were trampling us."

And he, moved by the passion that shone through her words, ran his hand over her shoulders, and told her that they would come back together, that they would fight in another way to deserve their country. What futile things one can say when young! They would always be united!, and, yet, that morning in the same Santa Maria del Popolo of thirty years ago he faced the fresco by Pinturicchio that she talked about so often on their honeymoon only to realize that it was stained with moisture, that the color had faded, like the joy of that moment, that he was married to a banal and detestable woman, who dragged along an even more banal and detestable stepson, that Eloísa Martínez was forever lost, that she certainly despised him with the same intensity with which he despised himself, that nothing was worth it.

"The Norwegian poetess. That's right … Sigrid Undset."

"The Swedish playwright, of course: Strindberg, the madman."

Enough! If there could only be silence again! If he could only enter again the candlelit chambers where there was no word, or

murmur, much less the din, but where only silence was nour-
ished. If they would only stop pursuing him! He awoke with
his eyelids wounded by the blinding light of September. It was
eleven; he looked for the exit and set out, unsteadied, to his hotel.

Rome, January 1962

WARSAW BOUND

If we are dreaming,
then let us dream until
our dream convinces us.
—Gabriela Mistral

for Zofia Szleyen

"'Tis good that at last your arrival comes tonight," she said, squinting her eyes; she pursed the corners of her mouth in such a way that her lips became a withered fold, a line, so thin as to be almost imperceptible, and allowed her head to fall on the glass, as if she were sleeping, as if she had suddenly died...

I looked at her in astonishment, not knowing for sure whether I had suffered a momentary blurring of my senses. Had she really spoken in Spanish, that squalid old sack of bony flesh whose figure, without being easy to explain why, was both victorious and macabre—stubbornly victorious, macabre by nature—or was she a mere hallucination produced by the fever?

The ice had crystallized on the window where she rested her head, forming a layer of dull sheen, a surface of icy fluff resembling the coat of a hare. She seemed to be unaware of the cold, ensconced in a coat of thick brown wool with black stripes, in a hood of timeworn golden fur, on which time, more than fade, bestowed an enviable patina, in her high, buttoned boots of slightly worn opaque suede, like the ones I had seen years ago in the sprawling ramshackle house of my childhood, in a trunk detested by my grandmother, but with which she never dared to part. *(Nothing should make me recall that time. You must go to Europe.*

43

Who hasn't spent good times there? You'll be a European; do you think I've not noticed it?; more than your brothers, you have the makings to be one. You'll while away your adolescence there, what some call the prime of youth. You'll go, but there are two places, which you are not to know, where no one will lay eyes only to come later and shatter my eardrums and senses with stories that I never ask for, knavish stories that I detest; I'll be happy and rest easy to know that you won't know them. There was a theater in Italy that no longer exists. I prayed, do you hear me, I prayed, on my knees until they hurt, until I was overcome with dizziness, that fire would rain down on it, that a spark from each of my prayers would catch and ignite it, destroy, smash to pieces that place where I suffered my indignity, where I overheard phrases that were not intended for me, claims that reason dictated were destined for me to hear, where, while he placed on his shoulders a green brocade cape, one of those brocades of an iridescent hue that we'll never see again, words trickled from lips that made her smile, that turned her eyes into blisters, which made me think that some encounters, that certain phrases that I had heard had not been casual; the other place, the most detestable of all places, that of my birth, hers, I need not even mention it. It no longer exists. It was only a bad dream, a poisonous mushroom that rose on the face of the world to nest shame and lasciviousness, to shelter them, to disguise them, but the fire, yes!, the fire, how I've rejoiced looking at the photo in the newspapers!, was responsible for washing the surface, purifying the air that we breathe today.)

A drunken young sailor tripped over the suitcase I had placed next to me, stumbled, and went on to fall beside the old woman, in the seat that had until then remained empty. The woman half-opened one eye; it was more like the opening of one of the many crevices that formed a wizened face crisscrossed by unforgiving furrows. He raised his head, shook the snow that was dripping from one side of his hat, and uttered, in a dry, unsparing tone, a spate of words that were incomprehensible to me. The sailor struggled to sit up again. The awkward grin that smirched his face could as easily be one of amends as one of ridicule.

I took a long drink from the flask that Juan Manuel had given me before I left Lodz. I delighted in how that mature liquor burned inside. I took another drink. The heat wave that spread throughout my body, as it diluted my fever into a general alcoholic torpor, allowed me to forget about the disease. My body was losing its tension. I was overcome by a general feeling of dejection: I wanted to cry, to sleep, on second thought, to die. I refrained from resting my head on the frost-covered glass, afraid that my fever would go up and that I'd end up mad before the trip arrived at its end. I used the last remnants of my clarity to curse myself for having boarded the train in such a state. What did it matter if I arrived in Warsaw the next day! What pressing urgency had caused me to race to the station that afternoon? Why did I have to board that car, where smoke permeated everything, where the heat was barely functioning, where the old woman took on the grotesque contours of a nightmare? I took another drink from the now almost empty flask.

The fever no longer worried me; my body continued to loosen up, become lost; I was barely aware of him, with the exception, of course, of his eyelids, whose weight seemed crushing; sleep would come. Sleep was all I could wish for; I even ceased to worry that, asleep, my head would come to rest on the frozen glass. Nothing mattered but closing my eyes; to bring to an abrupt end, to abolish, the blurred vision that surrounded me.

"You must have reached Warsaw in the autumn," I heard again through the shadows and my drowsiness. "It's a beautiful time of the year, I can assure you."

That woolen specter began to move ... a bony hand, the hand I had seen months before in Haarlem, in the Franz Hals Museum: the terribly emaciated, petrified hand of the regents of the Old Women's Almshouse, a claw clad in antique mountings, filigrees richly carved in dark silver, without the precious gems that must have once topped them off, emerged to secure with certain, nervous, and precise movements the thick, rich, anachronistic, and ridiculous traveling blanket in that second-class compartment, and put on gloves. The events from that moment on took on an accelerated, frenetic rhythm, an inverse ratio to the progressive weariness of my perceptions. The blanket was stored in a leather sack. The people stood, took down bundles and suitcases, began to circulate, and I suddenly found myself staggering, walking with a suitcase in my hand while the old woman's tenacious hook held my other arm. A sense of horror struck me intermittently as I wandered through deserted alleyways, splashing through the snow; she spoke without stopping, without allowing herself the slightest respite, in Polish, then suddenly in French, from time to time interspersing in a strained, almost imploring Spanish:

"He's going to meet you. It's a pity you drank so much, but even still he'll be happy. He's not seen anyone of his blood in all these years. I wanted to bring you before, but you went to Lodz, and now you've come back to see him, to be his joy, the sun that his winter needs ..."

It was the ditches, the snow-covered crags, scars left by the bombs that once flattened the city, the bombs celebrated by my grandmother, where I slipped time and again, and in which during one of many falls I lost my suitcase. The darkness made it hard to see, the snow fell in thick flakes, incessantly: Franz Hals' hand still clung to my arm, lifting me when I fell, rolling with me through the snow; always secure, stubborn in his haste. The wind cut our faces, caused the snowflakes to dance in the air, slowed the march. The lights of the city began to remain behind us. Were we walking along the banks of the Vistula? To where? In the depths of my soul I would have wished to have the courage to push the old woman away and escape her hook, her spell. But could I find my way without her guidance? To abandon her would have meant getting lost in that frozen night, surrendering completely to the winter lethargy of the earth, to cease to be.

We keep walking.

In the distance there was a rumble of voices; I opened my eyes, then, which the cold had forced me to half-close and turn down during the last part of the trek only to glimpse in the distance a pale light; as we drew closer I was able to make out a gateway in which two lads, in spite of the cold, were singing jazz and clapping rhythmically. As we passed they gave a mocking bow and spoke a caricaturesque greeting which the old woman did not return.

As we climbed the spiral staircase that jutted out from the building and that gave off a strong waft of cabbage stew, of misery, dampness, the old woman, that delirious vitality that she had displayed until then, seemed to abandon her. She deposited her bag in front of a door, helped me to lean against the wall, and inserted a key that was tied to her belt by a long cord into the lock.

"I don't trust them. Any of them; They showed up out of the blue, and little by little took over the house. At first they were more, some left over time. Like so many people, drunk, sinners of one or another kind. The only thing that can't be said about them is that they are cowards." She spoke nervously, sobbing, in a voice that was at the point of breaking; It seemed that speaking meant a possibility of escape, a flight. "They took over everything except this part that we kept. Tell me, what point could there be in preserving salons, terraces, gardens? What point in keeping a nursery and hothouses for palms and camellias that disappeared so many years ago?"

She attempted to straighten my hair with an icy, wet hand, to adjust the knot of my tie. I watched as she did it, without fear, without surprise, resigned.

Then, like a flash, she entered the dark hole that led to the door, only to resurface minutes afterwards with a candelabrum in her hand, in which a thick candle quivered. Inside me, feelings of horror were reborn and grew second by second. I felt assailed by a wave of unsuspected madness, by a complete havoc of the senses, by the collapse of reason. The conversations I held for two days in Lodz with my friends, in which we repeatedly affirmed our conviction of the rights of reason and the obligation to exercise it at every moment, seemed sad, ridiculous, wretchedly mocked by the unpredictable chain of events that marked and defined that night. All the talk and discussion about international events, about Cuba, about certain matters that concerned us, about Léger, whose retrospective I had just seen in Moscow, about Ehrenburg, Evtushenko, and Voznesensky, about Kott, Andrzejewski, Witkiewicz, Schulz, and Gombrowicz, about

Tadeusz Kantor, Grotowski, Wajda, and Penderecki, about Maria
Jarema and the last Polish abstractionists, only to end up here?

She drew the candle toward the photograph of a man whose
face was not completely unknown to me. With each of the old
woman's movements, the radius of light traced by the candle
changed, widened, diminished, grew in volume, traced frayed
brocades that hung from the walls, revealing the remains of once
sumptuous furniture. I was no longer myself; I fell into an arm-
chair that moaned under my weight. I plunged into a world of
cushions of thick, plush fabrics. She fluttered nervously from one
place to another; she lit two oil lamps that instead of light created
an atmosphere of ghostly chiaroscuro and accentuated the oddity,
the chaos of debris that characterized the place.

"They came like hordes; my nephew tried to protect me
with guards; he wanted to take me away from here, but I could
not leave *him*. I'll never leave him. I seldom go out; this time I
went to meet you, but I tell you that I seldom go out. My place
is here."

I didn't miss a word; amid the frenzy I listened with absolute clarity to each of her pathetically trilled r's. "You're the first.
I would have preferred, I swear to you, though no one would
believe it, even if he were the first to doubt it, for her to come,
but it wasn't possible; he loved her with a madness only comparable to mine, with the same passion, so when I learned of her
death I felt that a part of me died with her; more than inher-
itors of a common blood, we were the same person with two
distinct faces. She spoke with a passion that I only remember
having heard from another mouth, from other equally trembling
lips, from another similarly tormented expression; I recalled my

grandmother's last days, the final delirium from which her marriage in Paris emerged, a young Mexican attached to the embassy of his country in France, the meeting of the Creole family with the Slavic family, and a wedding trip through Italy accompanied by the all the family members, at the end of which she embarked for Mexico with her husband's people; of he, he, he who promised to catch up to her a few months later and who never did, an equally potent he on her lips, a he whom she had discovered one night at the theater after making a date with her sister.

"He wasn't the same when he arrived here. Those first nights the fire that consumed him thereafter began and whose embers were still in Venice, in Zagreb, in Vienna. When he arrived at this house—you could never imagine what he was like then!—I began to pick up the ashes. He became lost in a dream of coffee plantations, sunlit fields, foals, and ravines. A few winters later, I lost him forever."

I don't know what strength allowed me to follow her when, taking me by the hand, she led me to another more spacious, more untidy room, where the candle's light revived the specter of a grand marriage bed; we walked toward the fireplace from whose frieze she took a great bronze ciborium with the Mexican eagle laboriously wrought on top; she drew the candle close, and I could clearly read the name of my grandfather, lost during a night of theater many years ago, and a date: January 26, 1913.

"Do you see? His ashes just celebrated fifty years. No one of his blood has been with him, and now, as by miracle, you arrive." She put out the candle. I felt an intensely fine, sharp pain bore into the back of my neck; everything began to spin; the knowledge of it all was enough to cover a seemingly endless period of time in which I slowly fell, sliding down the body of the old woman who stood erect at my side; when my head hit her feet, everything ceased to exist.

Warsaw, January 1963

WESTWARD BOUND

for Bárbara Jacobs

Everything had become a constant disaster since the day he met his countrywoman and the young Venezuelan couple. Even before, though he was at least prepared and resigned to the fact: he knew whom he was dealing with. But Elisa and the two youngsters had caught him off guard, sorely abused his good faith, and ultimately launched him on the present course of torture that seemingly had no end. They began by describing the wonders of a trip by train; he would cross the whole of Siberia, an already classic journey, just think about it for five minutes, the Trans-Manchurian, the Trans-Siberian! They had made the trip (they claimed to have made the trip) a few months before and remarked that it was as a decisive experience in their lives. The words flowed as the four of them finished the bottle of strong Korean wine in which a coiled snake lay at the bottom.

"Go on, Doc, take the plunge, you've already had a good start; besides the trip by plane will only wear you out more, take a vacation, you've earned it. It'll be as restful as a trip by sea, but with the added advantage of being able to enjoy an endless parade of landscapes: one day the Gobi, the next Mongolia, where legions of camels run alongside the railway, then the Baikal, more like a choppy ocean than a lake, and all the Soviet republics, each one filled with a million curiosities; plus, it's very important since you work in finance to see with your own eyes—so no one can tell you later that it's this way or that way!—the real state of the economy of these countries; think about me for a second and sympathize with me, up to my neck in these Chinamen, who I can't manage to get along with to save my life." And the landscapes began to file by: lakes, forests, deserts, cities lost in the midst of thick forests, a Chinese restaurant and a European one, compartments with private bathrooms, several days during which nothing would disturb his rest, the landscape, yes, but through the window, while he, lying in his bed with a bottle of Scotch beside him, would recover from a hell of a trip through China, during which he had attended, as part of a delegation, the Canton industrial fair, and closed some excellent deals, even if it seemed that centuries had passed: the arrangements were very easy, an exchange in excellent conditions of chemical substances and materials prefabricated from surplus cotton, Henequen, mercury, and linseed. Very favorable compensation terms. Part of the transaction paid in pounds sterling. The other delegates left for Indonesia, from there they would fly to Europe; he, meanwhile, had to travel to Shanghai, then to Peking where he was to sign the agreements; of course, they were quick to inform him, it was merely a formality. A senior foreign trade official who was to sign the agreements was not in the capital at the moment, but had expressed his particular interest in welcoming him personally and hearing his impressions of possible future transactions, meanwhile he would be the guest of an association for the increase in trade with countries of Asia, Africa, and Latin America, that he considered it a pleasure to be able to be of service and to show him the characteristic sites of Peking, as well as the progress achieved by the Chinese people in recent years. And there began the over-whelming days that only came to an end with the signing of the agreements and that made him yearn like never before for the well-deserved, and highly appealing, vacations that Elisa and the young couple were proposing.

Truth be told, none of it has been real life. Where was the legendary and mysterious China? The unforgettable nights of Shanghai that young people everywhere have dreamt of? He had undoubtedly encountered a mysterious China, yet so unlike the one he longed for, and the nights in Shanghai had been unfor-gettable to the extent they were sinisterly tedious and fatiguing; his inseparable guides had led him to a humongous place where there were opera, puppets, and theater, and when, fed up and annoyed, because those little tunes were the same ones that had followed him relentlessly throughout the country, he suggested that they leave and look for a more exciting place, or, otherwise, take him back to the hotel, so they took him to another room in the same building where he sat in a small wooden chair, like a schoolboy in the middle of hundreds of schoolchildren, saw a middle-aged woman twirl madly in the middle of the stage, who, while casting a sneering glance at the audience, placed a hand on her neck as if to begin a striptease; when he believed that at last the spectacle was about to heat up a bit, the woman began to pull out from under her clothes bottles, pots, jugs, and even chairs, as if her meager body were a walking department store. Nothing about Orientals could be foreseen or known for sure, the proof being that when he commented to the Japanese industrialist with whom he shared a compartment (because the individual compartment, like the shower, like the two restaurant cars, the cosmopolitan travelers, the varied landscapes, the Gobi desert, Mongolia, and their herds of camels, various republics, had been a dream without the slightest relationship to reality) on his impressions about China, cautioning him that he didn't wish to broach the political situation, because if he shared his impressions, he would end up horrifying a lot of people, that he only meant to refer to the economic aspect, which concerned him strictly as a businessman, the Japanese man proved that the Asian in the end ends up always being one and the same—for him everything was reduced to smiles and to understanding English only when convenient and to offering him cigarettes or one of the oranges he was always eating with great enthusiasm—, and when he tried to make him understand his experiences in Peking, while those whoever-they-weres kept his documents, when more than guides or aides they turned into veritable torturers, at times taking him to an never-ending museum of the revolution whose visit lasted for centuries, at times to another one where amazing treasures were amassed in complete disorder, handfuls of giant pearls clustered in an icy tomb in the areas surrounding Peking, at times a dam, then visits to the Great Wall or a people's commune, which, with indescribable meticulousness, they make him walk the length of, then to a bookstore, a temple, a palace, a market, a park, and factories and factories, despite his contestations that he found none of it of interest and when, disgusted, he demanded his papers and refused to go on one more of those excursions that were draining his energy and his nerves and was irritated with the guide, the latter left, only to appear shortly thereafter accompanied by some other person, who sat, served tea, offered him a cigarette, smiled again, and explained in a very long speech, filled with furbelows and clichés, twenty thousand things that were beside the point, only to finish by concluding that the visit had to be made because it complied with the designated program, and when he told him that he was there only to await the signing of certain documents that for some Machiavellian reason were not being given to him and not for tourism, for which there were more appropriate places, that they should understand that every day he spent there he lost money, that in the West time served another purpose and use, hence the progress achieved there, that if the head of the Mexican delegation had said he could wait as long as necessary, it was only a figure of speech, and not for the perpetration of this abuse, the man left then still smiling, talking, talking, always talking, and the young guide soon reappeared, the latter very serious indeed, accompanied by a third person who recited a speech identical to the previous one only longer, emphasizing from time to time that the visits to the tractor factory, the model prison, or the Red Star Commune were noted in the program, and it was not appropriate to cancel them, until finally at the point of going mad, he left to visit the center of the popular arts to watch for hours someone cut colored papers or make pots, then visit later miles of another commune and the jail and listen in each place to mile-long speeches that could easily have been omitted since they were always the same, and if he made apologies for reasons of health, as had happened on one occasion, it was worse because he would end up at the hospital, where after three or four days of undergoing injections and blood withdrawals, it turned out that he had not even been spared the excursion, but that it had merely been postponed, "because it was so noted in the program," the Japanese man smiled good-naturedly as if he understood nothing and replied yes, they were indeed a great people and that he doubted very much that any other could combine so much wisdom and generosity in the way they extend hospitality to visitors, who every time he left China was pleasantly impressed, wishing only to have the opportunity to visit again, just as he also wanted to travel to Mexico one day and that he would surely find the opportunity, since his business, etcetera, etcetera . . .

What was one to do! They were of two worlds. He belonged irretrievably to the West; the morning he left Beijing he had felt it more acutely than ever; he was returning his room keys at the hotel when he was handed a postcard that had arrived at the very same moment, a greeting from Ramos from Paris; he announced that the delegation was on its way back to Mexico. As he gazed upon the sullen structure of Notre Dame, he was comforted, more than by Ramos' affectionate words, before that exquisite mass that stood illuminated beneath a blue that only the sky of Paris is able to boast; he boarded the train with the card in his hand, and placed it on the bedside table, then went down to collect the ridiculous bouquets of flowers with which they saw him off, and to hug his compatriot and the two youngsters, that trio who had rescued him in the final days and who made life more pleasant; they had explained to him an infinite number of matters regarding the eccentricity of these people and their experiences at the school where they taught Spanish; they had made him laugh hilariously once again, which he thought he had all but forgotten how to do, while they drank the snake wine that Elisa liked so much; he had won her heart out of pure nostalgia for their homeland but more than anything because of a woman's need, he had given her a ring with a pink pearl that he had bought on the last day at an antiquarian's house, and in the end she had been the worst trickster in the world, she had put him in that sort of big cage where he felt as if he were going mad, and the days went by with an unimaginable monotony without seeing anything but the snow, a constant snow that settled on the glass and prevented even the slightest contemplation of the landscape. He could not avoid the fainting sensation upon realizing that he could already be in Belgium and on a plane to Mexico as opposed to being three days and their respective nights out of Moscow. That morning when the Japanese industrialist reminded him that he would stay in Irkutsk and that he would make the rest of the journey by air, he thought he had seen an opening; he had wanted to do the same but had not been allowed; they explained to him that it was impossible because he didn't have a plane ticket; the Japanese man had bought his in Peking; he also lacked the proper visa; two stout Russians and the enormous woman who brought him tea in the morning and cleaned his compartment grabbed him by the arms when in a frenzy he tried to disembark; he returned prostrate to his lair, lay down on the bed, and looked at the photograph of Notre Dame, he thought not even then, far from the Chinese border, was he in his world, that his only world was that of the photo, but at that moment he had the impression that during those days of confinement the sky had become darker, Notre Dame appeared in a light that he had never seen, an absurdly artificial effect; it seemed to him that the photographer had mistaken the angle, that the chosen spot did not allow the building's total beauty to be admired, that the streetlight projected a light that robbed it of space, and that half the photo, the entire bottom part, was wasted. What was the point of portraying the street, the pavement?, or worse yet was that bench in the foreground with a man with his back to the camera; he felt a deep unease, a violent irritation, a pure hatred for the photographer who had committed such an infamy, then, anxious, he remembered that he had finished reading the detective novel that Elisa gave him before he left and took from his portfolio the other book that irrationally, perhaps only because it was written in English, he had bought from a secondhand bookstore in a Peking market. He read on the dirty cover: *The Priest and His Disciples*, by Hyakuzō Kurata, translated by Glenn W. Shaw, and he did not know what profound register was touched by those tiny lotuses drawn under the title or the Japanese hieroglyphs that decorated the cover, what's certain is that for some reason his hatred, his rage, his despair, the feeling of being in that compartment like a caged animal, disappeared, having been transformed into a gentle melancholy, a desire to complain about his luck, to lament in silence, and a need to find a shoulder on which to rest, and the fortune he was making, and his wife, his career, his office, the business conducted during the trip suddenly seemed like distant things that did not belong to him at all, the world to which he had aspired and always considered his goal was at that moment only a starting point bound for something, bound for something... He read two pages of the book, which left him fatigued, unable to penetrate that labyrinthine dialogue about death, sustained between a man and a *Being*, in which the *Being*, or however the word was translated, said:

"That's because death comes from sin. The sinless live eternally: The 'thing that dies' is identical with 'sinner.'"*

And the man asked:

"Then do you say that all men are sinners?"

"They're all bad. The price of sin is death," the Being answered categorically.

No, it was truly impossible to be entertained by such mystic-philosophical digressions. He slipped the Notre Dame postcard into the page like a bookmark and closed the book; he was exhausted, he began to sleep.

The next day he would arrive in Moscow. He had begun to feel a sense of hurry. He would save himself the three days he initially planned to devote to visiting the city, he would leave immediately for Brussels; if possible, he would do so that same night. He wanted to arrive in Mexico as soon as possible, he wanted to escape from that trip, from the memory of that trip, to go into his office to write reports, to dictate memoranda, to attend to his mail, to return to the normal rhythm of his existence. His stay in Peking had become eternal; now, however, it seemed to be summed up in a weekend crowded with remote events, lost deep in time, while the monotonous week spent on the train seemed infinite, although he had to confess that in the last few days he did not have such a bad time; perhaps it had been the Japanese man who irritated him, because since he had got off in Irkutsk, he found himself in a very placid mood, he spent most of his time in the compartment, which now belonged to him entirely, stretched out, resting, sleeping well; he tried again to read one of

---

* Hyakuzō Kurata, *The Priest and His Disciples*, trans. Glenn W. Shaw.

the detective novels, but it was impossible to enjoy them knowing already the plot and the outcome, so from time to time he turned to *The Priest and his Disciples*; he spent a long time reading the play's hermetic dialogues without trying to understand them, simply to kill time; that night he discovered that the weighty tome was more pleasant than he suspected. He put on his pajamas, picked up all his belongings, closed his luggage, with the exception of his attaché, and lay down on the bed. Finally the last night on the train! He opened the book at random and began to read the story of Kiyoshi Kawase, a student in a boarding school in Kyoto, who wandered this world as a mortal being for twenty-two years; he reveled, during such a short a time, in many of the fortunes of life, enjoyed the love of family and the other, was rich, and possessed a magnificent memory. Because of his talent his teachers and friends predicted great deeds; he tasted some misfortunes, all, but one, insignificant: he was afflicted by the heaviness of doubt. Around the age of nineteen, in the midst of his happy existence, he had fallen into this uneasiness: he doubted the reality perceived by his senses. One day, at the age of twenty-two, he was preparing for a test at school. He was leaving his room when he stepped back to look at himself in a mirror, and there, on the smooth surface, right beside him, a figure appeared, whose face was gradually beginning to resemble his own, though blurred, colorless, transparent. An enormous satisfaction, a great tranquility seized the young Kiyoshi, his doubt was removed, for the first and only time, he possessed a certainty; he had been usurping, with his habits, gestures, reflections, a role that was not his, he discovered that he was a ghost, that everyone around him were ghosts, that everything was spectral. Annoyed by his long delay, his teachers sent another pupil to look for him. When the latter reached the room, he found before the mirror, scattered and in disarray, Kiyoshi's clothes. A soft aroma of orange blossom floated in the room, mixed with another pungent odor that no one could identify.

He read the story deeply absorbed and was surprised that on the page following the disappearance of Kiyoshi, a dialogue continues with no relation to the story. He thought he had skipped a page, and after looking at the numbers he discovered that he had passed from page 62 to 93; he carefully checked the pages and soon noticed that the text he had read was a quinternion of another book sewn by mistake between pages 92 and 93 of *The Priest and His Disciples*, which is why it was written in the form of a story and not in dialogue like the rest of the play. When he examined the sheet, the postcard fell to the floor, he bent over to retrieve it to put it back between the pages of the book when he looked at it with nostalgia. Notre Dame seemed more distant than ever, unattainable; the lamplight illuminated the bottom part, the street. The streetlamp, the bench, the man facing backward, and next to him he noticed something akin to the shadow of another man; it seemed that the camera had moved at that moment and only managed to capture the specter of that man; he drew the postcard close to his eyes; the way he was sitting was familiar to him, the face turned to the camera was similar to his: not only that, it was his own, they were his gestures, the only thing that occurred to him was that in this life everything was nothing more than a joke. Never in all his life had he been afflicted by doubts, and yet, just as Kiyoshi Kawase, he came to discover that he was superfluous, though he could not make out whether he was living an existence already lived, or exactly where the usurpation lay; he grabbed his robe, left, walked cheerfully to one end of the car; there he ordered a large glass of tea from the portly waitress and returned to his compartment. He searched in his attaché for a bottle, opened it, drew a sedative to his mouth, then drank the tea. He crawled between the sheets to wait.

Warsaw, January 1966

THE RETURN

for Vicente Rojo

What would most surprise him later, when he remembered that day, was its extraordinary duration. If he could compare it to anything, it would be to his childhood days, when that little boy, wandering through a world of disorganization, feels and knows the true fullness of time, still free from the anxiety that time will trap and crush him. That Saturday would constitute a universe. He, who detests anecdotes, is suddenly full of them, a prisoner. He believes it ideal, both in life and in literature, that facts can be assembled, fused to such a degree that they become neutralized, diluted in a sort of fluid in which none of the parts is significant by itself but rather as part of the whole, which, after all is said and done, should be a mere climate, a certain atmosphere.

It hasn't snowed during the last week. The temperature varies between 40 and 42 degrees Fahrenheit, an extraordinary phenomenon in early February, and the clusters of snow on the sidewalks and roofs are melting. The thaw turns the streets into streams; at the entrance of the hotel large puddles have formed. The carpets ooze moisture. To top it off, during the last few days, a light drizzle continued to fall, and he, in his precarious state of health, his pathological propensity for colds, had to go from one end of Warsaw to the other in search of a place to live. After spending three weeks in bed, these outings are responsible for destroying the minute sense of balance he had attained with painstaking effort. It's almost two; the small square window contains the cheerless and opaque fog that surrounds the city. His head, his throat, his joints, all hurt terribly. The decline is total. He hasn't the slightest desire to go out. He calls Zofia on the phone to cancel the invitation to lunch; he explains how he feels. No, he doesn't know if he has a fever; he just put the thermometer in, but it almost certainly went up; it shows in the burning of his eyes, the choking. Not at all, I appreciate it, but there's no need to bother, and the maid has gone to order some food, it's just a matter of waiting a bit, he says two or three more sentences to reassure her and go backs to bed.

The objects themselves look different to him. They're the same, of course, but suddenly animated by an intention unknown to him. They're shadows; the depressing lead gray light that filters through the window deforms them, gives them a spectral appearance. He's drenched in sweat. He turns on the lamp. He looks, as if hypnotized, at the bar of mercury in the thermometer: 101.6. One shadow, the wardrobe; another, the desk. The usual disorder, accentuated even more by two weeks of confinement and disease, the smell of sweat, vodka. He gazes at objects at length, his clothes strewn about, his ties out of place; books, magazines, papers, all in disarray; he looks at everything deliberately as if he were trying to find in the objects the clue that would lead him to the dream from the night before. He had awakened stunned and wounded by the dream's violence, his forehead awash in sweat, and with an abominable feeling of guilt. It must have been early in the morning. Later, his gaze falls with renewed stupor on the thermometer. His fever continues to be the same as at the beginning of the illness. For two weeks the only thing they've managed to do is reduce it with antibiotics. The flu-like symptoms disappeared almost immediately; on the first day his fever had risen to 103.1; the following day, at night, thanks to the introduction of penicillin, it managed to drop suddenly to 96.8, and one day later it fell another degree and a half, leaving him so weak and lethargic that walking the few yards that separated him from the bathroom felt like torture. But later the fever returned, and the doctors couldn't explain the failure of the antibiotics and salicylates to reduce it; the bar of mercury told him that his body was bound to be harboring something intensely harmful, something that was breaking down so quickly that the medicines were unable to stop it. X-rays of the lungs and bronchi: everything perfectly normal; blood and urine tests; some results were still expected.

It occurs to him that perhaps they've discovered something incurable, which explains Dr. Adamowski's secrecy, the compassionate face of the ambassador when he brought him the boxes of food and drinks, the air of mystery that his friends assume, who must be in on the secret; he bundles up; begins to feel chills.

To make matters worse, days before, as he was beginning to feel better, the news that he had to leave the hotel had an ominous effect on him. A rumor had been going around for several months, which he had refused to believe. To be sure, on one occasion, he asked the ministry, and they answered that it was absurd, that he shouldn't even waste his time listening to people who were amusing themselves by creating difficult situations; they assured him that if the Bristol no longer wanted to house the fellows, the decision would apply only to those who were to come and not to the few who remained from previous years, who had, as it were, acquired rights. Nevertheless, it turned out that the rumors were true and that he had to leave; they informed him that they had secured rooms in family homes and he could choose among them the one that suited him best. He barely managed a response; he muttered that he was sick, asked for a few days to get back on his feet. He immediately began to call all his friends to intervene on his behalf. The results were fruitless. There could be no exceptions; the other fellows would protest. Three days later, he heard the same voice that urged him to investigate the available rooms.

"You run the risk," said the voice, "of missing out on the ones that are in the best condition, and, in the end, will end up finding yourself somewhere that's not entirely suitable."

That's why he'd gotten up, had walked every corner of Warsaw, wandering from one horror to another, enduring the whims of one landlady, the foul moods of another, the irritating paternalism of an old man who intended to prey on him as if he were his son and what's more charge him for it. At last, he agreed to move to a house in the Mokotów neighborhood.

He found it painful to leave the building. The Bristol had been his den for a year and a half, his refuge, his watchtower; a splendid time filled with people, adventures, friends, sorrows, readings, discussions, nights of absolute magic, golden sunrises, disastrous aspirin-laden mornings, furtive encounters, sullen days, intolerable revelations, surprises, summer evenings dedicated entirely to translation while contemplating with envy the freshness of the neighboring garden through the window, the undulation of bodies beneath the sun. The Bristol! The closing of this stage caused him almost physical pain. And under these conditions!

Someone knocks on the door. A waiter from the restaurant comes in with the food. Beside him, Marek. He ran into the maid, he explains, as he entered the restaurant. She told him that he was ill, and he decided to come up to keep him company. They would eat together. The waiter has also brought his order. When he's sick, he can barely tolerate Marek's presence. He aggravates his vitality, makes him feel even more diminished. That day he's coming to say goodbye; he's to leave that night for Zakopane, where he'll spend two weeks on holiday. He's in much less of a good mood than usual; at times, almost somber. He's in love, he confesses; he says with whom. Another surprise: Marek in love, taciturn and jealous, and during the entire time he's been dealing with it, he's been involved in one sexual encounter after another, which means as much to him as a good game of tennis or a morning swim in the pool. Not a single female tourist of interest has managed to escape him. He has fornicated with indiscriminate abandon with Scandinavians, Germans, Hungarians, and Latin Americans. In Zakopane, he's sure to feel better; he wants to get away for a while from bar life and devote himself for the time being to skiing. Perhaps they invited him to participate in wild boar hunt. The weather was perfect for it.

The piece of meat he brings to his mouth at that moment remains there for a short time, before being laboriously swallowed.

He sees a wild boar running. At that moment he thinks he remembers his dream but isn't sure; perhaps it's not the dream but the memory, pure and simple, of a real event that somehow relates to the dream that has left him so troubled. Amid a cloud of smoke, he sees a group of boys between eight and nine years old, armed with stones, clubs, bricks. There are at least five. They're shouting and making a racket. Their faces are dirty, reddened, and bathed in sweat. The heat that the spot gives off seems only to increase their determination, their excitement. They move along a metal pipe. They close off one of the openings with boards and throw stones into the other. One of them stokes the bonfire; they introduce the burning logs into the pipe. The smoke will make the animal come out and, indeed, a few minutes later, an opossum, confused by the fire, emerges. They scream like wild men, elated; they feel the hunter's excitement in their throats, their hands; their hours-long efforts have been rewarded. They beat it with bricks, with sticks, even with the burning logs; the opossum staggers, she's lost, falls, bleeds, emits a repulsive stench. But from her bosom, like small larvae, six, no seven tiny beasts emerge; blind, they stumble, barely making their way; the operation becomes easier, the tiny pissants offer no resistance; a few minutes later they're burning among the embers. The boys walk away with their arms locked around each other's necks, as in a round; they sing blithely, they know that the chickens the repulsive animal had been stealing will no longer disappear, they've done their good deed for the day. But that night, at home, when his dinner is served, he has to get up in a hurry and run to the bathroom to vomit. And now, many years later, the unexpected memory prevents him from eating the piece of tongue on his plate; he pushes it to the side with his fork and brings some rice to his mouth. He tries to find something of interest in Marek's conversation; he looks out the window: it's impossible to make out anything except the fog. The glimpsed scene, in all its detail, causes him to become lost in doubt as to whether opossums are marsupials or not; he doesn't know whether the female carried her children in a pouch, or if, pregnant, she gave birth as a result of the beating, the smoke, and the burns. He drinks his coffee in gulps, and asks Marek, just for the sake of courtesy, to stay a little longer; they'll listen to the record of Zarah Leander that he bought recently in Berlin. But Marek excuses himself; he still has to take care of some matters regarding his trip to the mountains.

He's alone. He lies down on the bed, rests his head on one arm, feels his pulse beating in his ear, caused by the fever. He tries to think about something. He doesn't want to leave the hotel, but the truth is neither does he want to stay; the only thing he finds appealing at that moment is not to exist; the flow of blood that he intuits in his ear drives him to the edge of nausea, as with any other organic process, with any anatomical confrontation, especially when, as on that day, he's so aware that his body harbors and conceals rot. He switched positions, but it doesn't ease the discomfort. A series of unpleasant scenes, all of which tend to suggest the great absurdity of his life, parade through his imagination, collide, become garbled. The senselessness and fatigue of such an endeavor. He doesn't want to go anywhere; the objects appear to be covered in a gray viscous light; their profiles, surfaces lose their smoothness, defined shape; he turns on the light, furious, and this seems to restore the material's normalcy. He thinks about calling Mercedes, his beloved countrywoman, so as not to be alone in the moments of prostration that lie ahead; he goes to the telephone, when he's about to call, the mere idea of having someone else in the room becomes intolerable. He takes a second aspirin and goes back to bed. The conversation with Marek has irritated him, he was left with the feeling that he had been stabbed in betrayal. He remembers that one day, not long ago, in a restaurant in the Old Town, Marek had told him that those people who made an altar out of love were ridiculous, grotesque. They had cited examples, had laughed out loud, and now he's consumed the entire lunch in mourning for an ill-fated love. Just then, he feels a nasty jealousy—if only he could also feel a connection with someone! Over the years he has suffered a kind of emotional barrenness that eats away at everything; his very friendships bring out a very superficial tension in him, and in no way create internal demands.

He imagines the rain through the window. He'll have to be locked up in that foul-smelling room for the next few days, drenched in sweat, annoyed, with no appetite for work or reading. More weeks like the last few, with money that doesn't arrive from Mexico, and while people pester him to move out of his room and go live with one of those harpies he visited and begin life as a boarder, which he has always shunned. The weariness brought by the fever causes him to despair, his eyes hurt, he can't read, listening to music annoys him, the idea of receiving visitors while he's unable to clean up or air out the room disgusts him. Everything becomes an uphill battle; not knowing how to revive the old notion that has sustained him on other occasions: to disappear, to fold his death into mystery. The reality of dying doesn't frighten him, but he is horrified by the possible comments about his suicide. It was a pleasure that he would not give to certain relatives and friends who would claim to have always predicted that end, "after all, the path he chose was inevitably going to end like this." He would walk into a forest, lie down somewhere, and allow the snow to finish him; no one would ever know what he was doing there. Impossible to talk about suicide.

The phone rings, he lets it ring—one, two, three, four long rings—without lifting the receiver; he's certain it's the woman from the fellowship office calling to urge him to move out of the hotel. He takes off his pajamas, dresses rather haphazardly, slowly. His movements are difficult; he places, out of habit, some books in his satchel and leaves. He says hello to no one in the lobby; he leaves the key and departs as if in a hurry, as if someone were chasing him, he goes out into the street and hails a cab to take him to the train station.

His head is about to burst; he wants to hurry events along, to end everything once and for all; his throat barely allows him to swallow his saliva. He walks around the main hall, in the midst of people scurrying, shaking off the snow, groups saying good-bye. He moves, as if sleepwalking, toward a window, gets in line; when it's his turn he asks for a ticket to the German border. He'll get off at a village near the dividing line and enter a forest; in his current debilitated state, the cold will make short work of him; the following day they'll find his body. The clerk hands him the ticket, he asks about the next train, it will leave in six hours. He stumbles out onto the street, he doesn't know how he has fallen into such a puerilely macabre plan. It terrifies him to think that if a train had been about to leave, he would have boarded it and allowed himself to be carried away by the rhythm of events; his teeth chatter, he can barely control the trembling of his knees. He has to wait a long while in the elements for a taxi; when he returns to the Bristol, standing in front of the great Venetian windows, the person entering looks like a mere specter, the ghost of himself. In the lobby, as he asks for the key, someone approaches him, it's Zofia, who's accompanied by another person, undoubtedly a doctor: she explains that after having spoken to him on the phone she became very worried; an hour later she called back and no one answered; she rang management and they told her that he was in his room so she imagined that if he hadn't answered it was because he felt very bad. She had brought a doctor. Why on earth had he gone out in this weather! Only a madman would have had such a notion! He apologizes, says he only went to the pharmacy. They go upstairs, the doctor examines him, whispers something to Zofia, they then explain to him that he's very ill, that he must be admitted that very night to a hospital. He hears his friend begin to make the arrangements over the phone. He's burning with fever.

"It's all arranged. Unfortunately, I won't be able to stay with you. I have an urgent matter at my sister's house. Our lawyer will meet you there. I'll drop you off at the hospital. You'll give them these papers."

They go downstairs. He can barely see, remain conscious. He finds himself seated on a wooden bench in a room covered with white tiles where Zofia has left him. A nurse comes out, collects the papers, tells him to sit down again. A woman beside him wrings her hands. Inside, the screams are terrible. Veritable shrieks of despair, of madness. He knows that if they continue he will also begin to howl.

"It's my sister," the woman next to him explains. "She has fits."

He wonders why they don't come to attend to him. Why have they left him there, in that senseless waiting room?

"I studied English for seven years, and I can't say a word," the woman continues on learning that he's a foreigner. "Seven years! But that's just the way I am ..."

He begins to laugh. He sees a kind of string of stones, braided rock clusters. He struggles to know what it is, those interwoven rocks that contract and expand and that in some way tell him that he is there and then, that he's still alive. He notices that the thousand theories in which he has taken pleasure during the last years, explanations, justifications, presumptuous interpretations, collapse and remain at his feet like fallen leaves, he's heard screaming that he wants to return to his homeland, to his house, his childhood, for them to leave him alone, that he wants to return, die, lose himself there. He manages still to see a nurse working diligently at his side; in his vein he feels the needle that will restore him to the night.

Warsaw, February 1966

ICARUS

for Roberto Echavarren

That evening at a showing of the Venice Film Festival the narrator saw a Japanese film that depicts, in an apparently unambiguous way, although the action transpires in Japan (and an episode take places in Macao), the life of a friend who died a few days ago under strange circumstances in a small city on the coast of Montenegro. He walked around, shaken, for several hours, returned to his hotel, telephoned Mexico, spoke to his wife, but nothing has been able to ease the distress caused by the final scene.

Everything exists to ensure his peace of mind and relaxation. Capable hands, provident eyes, minds designed exclusively to anticipate his every need and desire and to attempt to satisfy them have endeavored to create that atmosphere, so necessary in those moments when a reaffirmation becomes indispensable. The telephone within reach; thick brocade curtains; a creased cretonne bedspread with soft green stripes that matches an even softer, almost imperceptible one; a Guardi reproduction, another by Carpaccio. Chrome or aluminum appointments dispersed judiciously among the dark furniture. Everything to the extent necessary to remind the traveler that he's not alone, that he hasn't fallen into another time, that the Carpaccio and the Guardi and the faux brocade that cover the walls are merely ambience, that he occupies his century, that one of the doors leads to a bathroom where the tile, the plastic, the metal plating, all sparkle. To remind him, in the end, that with the simple push of a button a waiter will appear and that, minutes later, a whiskey, ice, and, if he wishes, a good *risotto di pesce*, *cassata*, and coffee will appear on a table.

Carlos would speak at length about the advantages that living in a hotel could provide. In reality, he spent a good part of his life in them; he was familiar with the entire gamut, from that kind of hotel to the seedier boardinghouses, rooms-for-rent of an indescribable look and smell. Namely, like the place where he had spent his last days must have been! In the movie there was a large, dilapidated two-story wooden house; the bedrooms were on the upper floor, rectangular rooms with six or seven broken-down beds. In a tearoom downstairs, townspeople met to discuss current events, play cards, pass the time. It rains nonstop. The torrential rain forms—in *Rashomon*-esque style—a solid curtain, thick and gray, that isolates both the people and the objects themselves. The hotel is almost empty. It's off-season, and he's the only guest in his room. The humidity and cold torture him; cause him to feel permanently ill. He has called the landlady several times to show her the two leaks in the ceiling, but the old woman merely grimaces and does nothing. He ends up putting a laminated pot under one of them and a towel under the other; from time to time he gets up to wring out the towel through the window. He gathers the blankets from the other bed to cover himself. Days pass with periods of intermittent exhaustion. He spends hours in bed huddled beneath a mound of covers; the only thing he can think about are his hands, frozen stiff by the cold. He has the look of a sick animal, at times moaning softly: an animal curled up to die. And he knows that winter has just begun, that he must withstand nature's cruel joke for long months, and that the worst months are yet to come. He opens a container, chews some crackers smeared with something resembling a fish paste that he moistens in a glass. He does calisthenics in an attempt to warm his body; sometimes he takes his notebook and goes down to the tearoom. The three or four peasants who come there barely speak; the dark and cold bring them together, isolate them. He's worried about running into the other boarder and her grandson; days before she had sat beside him and unleashed a nauseating screed about her ailments; diarrhea, colds, punctures, nerves, her liver, the pus that won't stop, shots, enemas, sulfur baths. The only thing visible through the window is a dark blanket of rain. The camera masterfully recreates that world of darkness in which there is an occasional sudden flash of light: drops ricocheting off the sidewalk like bullets on a metal surface, an old, dark jalopy driving across town in the middle of a cloudburst. Behind the car, a destitute poet wrapped in a threadbare overcoat that goes down to his feet quickly makes his way; he flails his arms as if battling the very substance of life. On a table, next to an iron stove whose heat seems to benefit no one, the obese protagonist (how distant now from the elegant young man from the passionate scenes in Macao!) attempts halfheartedly to jot down a few lines in his notebook, but the ideas don't flow. He writes a few sentences, crosses them out; the pen begins to dance, to stutter, he traces lines, draws flowers and outlines of women, numbers, he stops; he begins again the task of outlining the paragraph whose progress has been painstakingly slow. In the end, he tears out the page, wads it up, and throws it away. He orders a bottle of liquor and fills a glass. At that moment, soaked and trembling, the old bard bursts into the bar.

It's obvious that the use of light serves a symbolic function.

The psychological atmosphere, at least, intensifies and diminishes with its help. In the opening scenes, during his youth, the sunlight is radiant and becomes increasingly stronger until the scenes in Macao where the brightness at times becomes unbearable. Everything contributes to it, not just the sun beating down on the characters; the sheer, pale suits of the extremely beautiful actress, reminiscent of Paz Naranjo, the young men's hats, the cream-colored awnings of the street cafés.

"This light is blinding," he says as he boards.

Later, the light slowly fades until disappearing almost entirely in the closing scenes: the fishing village where the protagonist has ultimately taken refuge. The sun, the few times it appears, is like a sad parody. There is nothing but fog, rain, and cold: a grayness that falls from the sky stains the rosettes and seeps through the walls. A damp cloud hangs in the air and surrounds the few patrons in the tearoom.

He remembers something from the last letter. Could it still be among his papers in Mexico? It was a long letter, whiny and irritating. He spoke of the melancholy that had taken over the tiny city as fall yielded to winter, of the darkness and rain and lack of incentives, of the scarcity of people to talk to. Of his recent encounter with an old, toothless poet with a long, thin beard who preferred the loneliness of a hideout on the mountain; he was his only companion, not a traveling companion because the weather no longer allowed it ("the bloody cold has dug its claws into this place, which until last week was like an endless sun paradise that existed outside the laws of weather. Suddenly, at dusk, a brutal chill began to descend from the mountain..."), but a drinking companion, a tavern mate.

No matter how many times he attempts to go for a walk, to lose himself, to unload on his friends, to be absorbed by the city, to read a little, to sleep, to think about the phone call with Emily, the movie continues to obsess him; it awakens his guilty conscience. He thinks that he and other friends should have made him return to Mexico, wired him a ticket, put him in an alcohol treatment clinic if that's what was needed; anyway, something certainly could have been done, anything, besides leaving him to die in that forsaken town, forgotten by everyone. He must arrange a meeting with Hayashi, the Japanese director, to find out how he was able to know those final details; to tell him, even though he won't believe him (like a good Oriental he will pretend and smile politely, but without completely hiding an expression of boredom) until he begins to give him names and details, he will have to tell him that he wasn't just a friend of Carlos, but rather he is the original of the somewhat absurd boy, the confused young man who appears in one of the movie's passages, the one who for one night, for a few short hours one night, was the real lover of a real women who was alive now, if in fact she was still alive, decrepit, fussy, obstinate in her dislike of Carlos, confined to an upscale clinic on the outskirts of London. He wants him to say whether Charlie's death, the circumstances of which no one ever knew, was just as the movie describes. He will add (if he only had that letter to show him!) that he knew about the existence of the ragtag old man who turned his back on literary fame to go to live in a shack in the mountains, could he please explain what his last weeks were like in the Bay of Kotor.

Because in the film, after the first encounter between the two men of letters, the visits become more frequent, always in the tavern next to a window not far from the fireplace, where they watch the rain. The first time, the poet walked toward the stove, leaving a watery stream in his wake. He sat at the table beside the protagonist, the alleged Carlos.

They exchange a few words; something leads them to identify themselves as writers; they talk a little about literature, many of the place's pros and cons, the landscape, and also about their dreams, aspirations, projects. They're like two boys intent on conquering and changing the world, art, literature, life, no less! (*Non, Jef, t'es pas tout seul!*) They clink their glasses frequently; they consider themselves brothers, confrères, poets, misunderstood by the times they live in; in one breath, they curse their era, in the next they proclaim it extraordinary, seminal, something yet to come. A grand era in spite of the fatigue and ennui it has produced.

And one day he confides to him that he's having problems; he tells him about his misfortune, about the check that hasn't come. The landlady has threatened to confiscate his luggage and throw him out of the hotel; he doesn't know what to do, he doesn't even have money to send a telegram. He'd like to sell some clothes, but he doesn't know anyone in town. The poet assures him that he won't get much for his suits; but the watch, on the other hand, could bring a large sum. But he refuses; he explains that it was a gift; besides, not knowing the time makes him uneasy, it causes him to feel dizzy and sick to his stomach. The poet insists. He assures him that he'll have the money in less than a half hour. Finally, he hands over the watch, waits, and falls into a deep depression. He's certain that he's been cheated, that he'll be thrown out of the boarding house; the watch was the only thing he could rely on to pay a driver to return him to civilization; when the other man comes back with the money he can scarcely believe it. They call for the landlady and pay his bill; he has a few coins left. They order a bottle of liquor, then another. They get drunk. The protagonist listens to the toothless old man, dirty and scruffy beyond description. Even in the moments of greatest camaraderie, he continues to provoke in him a certain degree of disgust (since, in a way, it's like seeing himself reflected in a mirror that offers him a glimpse of the future, an image that's hot on his heels). He concocts—in great detail, and with a vast display of grimaces and guffaws that expose his gums and what's left of his rotting teeth, with winks that cause his entire face to move to the point of forming a crossword of wrinkles, and dirt and hair—a future free of financial cares. He listens to him—at first with amazement, then with a trembling desire to participate, finally with enthusiasm—narrate his experiences in that cabin where he writes when he pleases, free of worries, and from where every now and then he'd go down to town to buy a newspaper, although now he did it more frequently to converse with him, since he didn't usually meet people from the city, much less of his quality, and he invites him to share his house. There he'll find the peace he was looking for and will be able to finish that novel that he's told him about so many times.

They continue to drink.

Then, stumbling, unsteady, they go up to the room. With the poet's help, he gathers his things and places them in his suit-case, wadded-up clothes in disarray, cans of food, a pair of canvas shoes; they pack his books, folders, papers, all strewn about the room, in a basket that they cover with newspapers. Later, under a fine rain and in the middle of the darkness, they walk along the town's long, narrow main street (the only one), that runs along the coast. They start up the mountain along a rocky path. The rain blinds them at times; stumbling here and there, they shout curses and stop to catch their breath. They pass the bottle back and forth. Both, but especially him, are completely drunk. They continue to walk. At last, his friend's hut appears, rickety stacked rocks, fragments pulled from the mountain itself, covered with a straw roof. The poet pushes open the door and invites him to go in. At that moment, as if struck by lightning, he understands everything. He looks at the pile of wet straw they will share that night, the remains of a fire, the dank dirt floor. He realizes, with unspeakable horror, that life has caught up with him, that the future that fate had woven for him had unraveled. He knows that the old codger was the bait that led him to the trap, that the world was finally able to get rid of him, to dot—and with such accuracy!—his i's, to eliminate him once and for all. He knows he won't be able to live in that pigsty, but that he won't be able to return to the hotel either, that he's moved beyond that stage. The modest rooming house is now as inaccessible to him as the restaurants in Tokyo, the beautiful garden of his house in Macao, his paintings, his good tailor, champagne. He knows that from the next day on, he'll have to look for dry branches to warm himself, that he's become the poet's servant. From time to time he'll go down into the town to beg and buy food and alcohol. To the people there he'll be just another madman. His teeth will also rot. He leaves the cabin, begins to run, and takes the wrong path. The rain has once again begun to pour. He runs alongside the cliff, slips, lets out a brief cry, rather a moan. The basket floats on the water. Icarus has once again drowned in the sea. In the meantime, in the cabin, the poet rifles through his suitcase. Ecstatic, he tries on the pants, the shirts, a sweater; he delights in smelling the bag of tobacco.

For the moment, the memory of that scene makes him feel the need, the urgency to hear Emily's voice again. He's about to make another call to Mexico. But after a moment of hesitation he decides that it would be senseless to call a second time, it would give a false impression. The best thing, then, will be to go to bed, try to read a little, take a Luminal, fall asleep at a decent hour. He knows the next day will be awful. His schedule is full of appointments, from morning to night. He won't even be able to talk to Hayashi. It'll be better to leave it for another day. In the end, what difference would discovering a new detail about Carlos's death make? He pressed the lamp button. Gaurdi's landscape, Carpaccio's prostitutes, the brocade, the Towers of Trebizond on the night table, the telephone, were all absorbed into the darkness. He's exhausted. He places a hand beneath the pillow and immediately falls into a sleep that erases all his fatigue, the shock, the guilt or rancor that the disjointed day had caused him.

Sutomore, November 1968

THE WEDDING ENCOUNTER

for Jorge and Lali

In Portinatx, north of Ibiza, above an anthill of barely visible, almost imagined inlets, he reviews the notes for a story project sketched months ago about an also barely divined experience, as dark as the landscape that stretches beneath his balcony: a thick mantle, whose bosom is sometimes uncovered by instantaneous illuminations: the flash of lightning reveals that the darkness behind the glass is only the last of many layers of the same substance, thick as a lead emulsion, that becomes lost on the horizon. There is no blue sea, rather dirty water, as dirty as the sky.

A pang of boredom leads him to review the notes for a final short story project. The need to write it had been so pressing that for a few days he was unable to enjoy any movie, book, meeting with friends. All he wanted was to sit in front of a notebook and outline his architecture. That's why he put aside that other confusing story with which he was struggling at the time: that of a frightened little man who, dressed always in a shirt of a purple velvet, raced through the city from one side to the other, from La Barceloneta to the slopes of the Tibidabo, from Sants to San Andrés, trying to escape a hypothetical pursuer, attempting to protect himself under the wing of the pair of old women whom he took turns in guiding through the city; two ghosts visiting an old dwelling, two women altogether different except in their need, the obsession to cling to a part of the past with which to face an old age that is collapsing on them. The little man will become their cicerone and by their side he will find some of the protection he so desperately needs. One of them was in another time a war correspondent; she returned to Spain to consult archives and libraries, more than anything to collate images, to remember, to make sure that she has lost not only one—that one—but every battle. The day of her farewell, the day when the man in the violet shirt is going to sink back into his viscid helplessness, she takes him to a corner of the Avinguda Diagonal, where she recounts to him the departure of the brigades.

"We were sure we'd be back shortly. It seemed that the entire population had accompanied us. It had to be a strategic retreat, we thought. It was impossible, it was too cruel to accept that we had lost the war."

The other had lived in Barcelona from 1943 to 1945. One day they drank like madmen. Drunk, she began to remember her husband. They stopped at a thousand tin-pot bars: at last they went to the seedy part of the city, and in one moment, on a corner, before a door, she shouted excitedly:

"This was the best date hotel I've ever seen in my life. You have no idea how luxurious it was. By this door we women entered; by that one, the men." Then, upon noticing the surprise in her protégé's eyes, she added, hastily: "I used to meet my husband here. We liked to play; give each other certain surprises."

But neither the political adventures of the one nor the erotic ones of the other would succeed in freeing him from his harassment.

That story, a short novel, had demanded too much effort from him, required greater knowledge about the city than he possessed. Somehow his pursuit had to fuse with his architectural vision of Barcelona, with which he ran the risk of becoming bogged down in the folklore of Chinatown or in modernist paraphernalia, blinded by mere surfaces. In any case, the truth of the matter was that the story of the pursued man and of the old ladies whose skirts he didn't dare to let go was ruined by the violence of another startling event, an excitement that, unfortunately, suffered the same fate as all the projects of the last three or four years. When in Portinatx he rereads the sketches of the story that took the place of the little man's, he thinks about the necessity of accepting his destiny and conforming to the modest role of literary commentator that he has been playing.

On that occasion, as always, he has traveled with a suitcase filled almost exclusively with his fake work implements: a few notebooks—on several occasions he has come up with the idea of writing a travelogue—, several books that he will not read, except the routine vacation detective novel, this time by van Gulik, and a folder filled with letters to answer (already on the very day of his arrival he wrote to Victoria to tell her about the amazing experience of his night on the ship, a true ship of fools, packed with a youth among whom he felt like a mummy, surrounded by guitars, long hair, and bright multicolored clothes, in the bosom of a deafening Children's Crusade that, having traveled the roads of Europe, boards the ship to Ibiza, the last anchorage before arriving to the Promised Land. What perhaps impressed him most during the voyage was the radical discrepancy between the possibilities of pleasure available in his adolescence and those enjoyed by the swarm he is contemplating with envy, leaning on a rail. He moves his gaze around the various groups on deck. A German woman, who could have been his classmate at the Mascarones school, strolls with martial and inquisitive gestures among the crowd. The sloppiness of her attire and her demeanor remind him of a certain jocular character from his university years. The horror that the scene produces in him surpasses chronological infamy; the difference is not reduced or explained by the mere passage of twenty years; it is something more radical; the intrusion of a certain zoological element into the cage of a distinct species. As if, suddenly, in the pavilion of the wading birds, among flamingos, white and pink herons, storks and cranes, amidst a luxury of silky, oiled plumage, a hyena had snuck in. But he needs to make that repulsive, gelatinous experience swallowable; that's why, upon writing to Victoria, he prefers to comment that he had the feeling that a mole had entered the cage of the herons and— what could he do!—he concluded that they were animals with the same right to the landscape, to the sea, to the sun. He writes that first letter shortly after getting settled in the small hotel in a spot discovered at random from a card bought a few minutes after landing in Ibiza; on it Portinatx appeared as a hodgepodge of bays, coves, and inlets. His arrival coincides with the start of the rainy season. A large part of the time he's a prisoner in his room, just like, so it seems, the Rojas, the Uruguayan couple he met the day he arrived and with whom he would like to spend more time, in an attempt to escape from a group of Dutch whose impertinence obliges him to write several letters, not only to Victoria, but also to Isabel, who embarked with him on the trip, to Carlos, to several aunts, to many cousins, to the Martinellis, to Miklos, without his activity ending there, since in the eleven ensuing days he will possess an amount of free time as he has not enjoyed in years. In addition to the novel by van Gulik, he reads most of the books stacked on the bedside table and leafs through the notebooks in which supposedly he's to write down his travel impressions, in which he finds the notes, the different beginnings of that story for which he may one day find the proper form. He doubts that day will come. The time to choose has passed, and he chose the wrong direction. Moreover, in that particular case, the obsession that for a few days prevented him from taking an interest in everything that was not the subject has disappeared. At that time, obsessed by the two marks he saw on his chest, he tried to establish a literary construction that not only would free him from that image, but also raised, by mere intellectual curiosity, certain questions of literary technique. To blow up the coherence in his characters, the rhythm, the development of the subject, for example. It occurred to him that the lips, the teeth, and, above all, the laughter of the sailor were basic elements on which he should linger deliberately, to the point of creating a gravity that weighs on the rest of the story.

But if his purpose had been the elimination of a personal tension, he could be proud of having succeeded. It vanished like other figurations that revolved around it. And now he only finds in a few paragraphs in the process of being developed two or three elements that seem suggestive to him: the waiting woman, the absent lover, the mutual friend who lives through the experience, images of boats run aground or sunk. One of the notes alludes to three flies caught in a spider web, three flies capable of turning of their own accord into spiders, surrounded by flies condemned to be only flies, whom the others could take prisoner and devour whenever they wanted. And, dismayed, he thinks that when the moment of change presented itself in which those images attempted to thread together into a weave, when each thread was to be intertwined with the others to create a coherent figure, he fell apart, already defeated. He had furiously applied himself to the task, but as the story became clear, when a definite effort was required, he neutralized it and put it down in the most idiotic way, by preparing ill-defined essays on the Italian novel of the nineteenth century, which in reality interested him very little, or worse, by going to the movies, which always succeeds in distracting him, without having to worry too much about what he's watching, and so he spent his time, and the various beginnings of the story did not go beyond being vague notes about trapped flies, ships, and shipwrecks. On the other hand, notes on Manzoni, Capuana, D'Annunzio, and Verga abounded.

But in the staleness of Ibiza, by inertia, he falls into the temptation of returning to work on that story, and with that intention, interested more than anything in the phenomenon of the charge and discharge of an energy different from the others, a night in which he chats with the Rojas in the hotel restaurant, he tells them that when he believed himself to be a writer, when—he corrects himself immediately—he was an active one, he began to experience those tensions accompanied by a pressing need for expression, which gradually faded after not finding an immediate response. He also points out that in recent times, when these alterations occurred, consciously or unconsciously, he began to resist them, withstanding their pressure flat out. Instead of writing and freeing himself from them, he fought off neurasthenia for a few days until, thanks to his articles, to the various tricks that composed his daily life, and, above all, to the movies, he once again felt free. Was there any difference between obsession and inspiration? Either he or Rojas or Rojas's wife remembers that when someone asked about inspiration he said he did not know what that meant, that someone else stated that ninety percent of literature was dedication and discipline, ten percent talent, and zero inspiration, but neither do they remember the author of the phrase or the exact proportions; the only thing they are sure about is that perseverance was the largest slice and inspiration none, or an insignificant one. In an attempt to provide examples for her points of view, she brings up the famous picture of the muddy drawers of the little girl who's climbing down from a tree, which prompted Faulkner to write a masterpiece, and then Rojas, to his surprise, because during earlier conversations he had not expressed the slightest interest in questions of literary theory, sketches in a calm and parsimonious voice, as if he had suddenly become his teacher, a historical development of the concept of inspiration, starting with "Sing, O muse, the anger of Achilles son of Peleus," where the poet, the simple spokesman of the muse, is therefore an inspired, possessed man; he then jumps to the Renaissance, which resurrects the concept, and to the moments of the romantic frenzy in which to doubt inspiration is to commit a sacrilege of dimensions comparable only to the oafish fatuity of blindly trusting in reason, and then to Dario's assertions and Huidobro's theories, without giving him the slightest opportunity to express his views, not even to express his agreement or dissent, because he barely attempts to say anything, the other man stops him with a dry:

"Yes, perhaps, I'm not sure; I should be better informed so I can opine."

And he notices that he indeed knows very little, so little that he cannot even pinpoint the concept he's trying to develop. Obsession! Inspiration! That night he returns to his room with several cognacs under his belt, convinced that both the Muse and the deity who seeks perseverance have turned their backs on him, distraught like an old collector forced to part with the last of his paintings, knowing that the moment in which inspiration arrived will not be repeated, that the liberation had been realized by incorrect means, less compromising and entirely spurious, without requiring any effort outside of creating a vague awareness of guilt, frustration, personal betrayal; although he should specify that he sometimes remembered with nostalgia the framework of that abandoned plot for which he had already established a general outline, the determining situations that lead the protagonist to assume the situation of his friend, which, without scarcely noticing, makes her aware of a personal yearning, uncovers in her unsuspected desires, begins to upset her in that ship-like hotel where she awaits the letter from her lover. Madness should appear now during a dream, at the moment when the identity of the body being whipped is revealed to her.

The notes of the story he finds in the notebook were like a kind of rehearsal held in vain, because the concert, due to the absence of a conductor, or perhaps, of a score, was never held. He reads a few pages from when he began to integrate the elements of the narration.

"The story must be told by the woman or by an impersonal narrator with a specific point of view, a focus of consciousness.

Everything will begin in earnest after her conversation with Javier. At first the protagonist feels obsessed with knowing what the sailor is like physically. What would a native of Ufa be like? To locate on the map said Republic of Bashkiria. Her friend, the decorator who has lived the adventure, comments: 'By his hair I could see that he was a Slav.' How far did Javier go? At what point had he stopped? He must have struck him. How else could he know that he smiled when he was whipped? How did he treat him now? She'll stop seeing him for a few days until she can digest the story. But the story doesn't allow itself to be digested, rather, on the contrary, it gradually possesses her, it will end up devouring her. She sees it even in her dreams. When Javier tells her the incident about the glass of beer thrown to the floor, she comments: 'Sure, he throws it, so they'll hit him.' There are moments when he would like to go look for him around the port. Would it be hard to find him? He has some information: a German boat, registered in Hamburg. Boris, born in Ufa, resident in Hannover. Ufa, yes, like the company that produced Zarah Leander's movies. Who is she? What is her profession? Journalist? But, then, what is she doing locked up in that hotel in Barcelona? She could have been a journalist when she met Jimmy and quit her job to go away with him. From time to time she sends an article to Caracas. Josefina and Javier are Venezuelans. She detests her name; she prefers to be called Fina. For months she has been waiting for Jimmy to return to the hotel, which looks like a ship to them. Perhaps they are the only ones who see the likeness. But the wait cannot be months, rather only a few weeks. Since she's lived with Jimmy he has only been unfaithful to her a few times. They both believe in sexual freedom but rarely practice it. This point may not mean anything. On the other hand, it is essential to point out from the beginning that she has always suffered from some nervous illness."

In writing those notes, he began to know what path the plot would follow. There would be three characters: the waiting woman, the absent lover, the decorator friend. At first he thought of making him a painter, but decorating, if only because of its obviousness, was more appropriate for the experiences he was to live. When he had the protagonists more or less sketched out, he noticed that they didn't matter, that they were archetypes that life repeated cyclically, that even though it was painful for him to accept the assertion, the only thing that mattered was the story. Any struggle against the anecdote was already lost.

Another note:

"The passion of the absent one, Jimmy, for the sea, is boundless. Fina knows from the start that the sea is her only rival. The sea and ships. He may also be an occasional journalist. He has other earnings, other sources of income. He's written several travel books. They usually spend half a year in each place, sometimes less; they then undertake another long journey. Always by boat. From La Guaira to Yokohama, from Yokohama to Vancouver, from Vancouver to Cape Town, from Cape Town to Barcelona. Jimmy would like these journeys to never end. They have traveled on Norwegian, Greek, Yugoslav, German freighters. The last voyage—for her extremely exhausting—was done on a Liberian-flagged ship whose crew looked like the dregs of the international navy, a bunch of harrowing adolescents, or old former legionaries who looked at her with a strange glint in their eyes; she now knew that it was not the product of desire. Could there be many men in the world like Boris, the sailor with blue bovine eyes who worked on a German ship? It was a hellish trip. At times it was almost impossible to conceal her spleen, to conceal her resentment at seeing Jimmy reborn at the mere contact with a ship, at the first mouthful of salty air, at the characteristic stench of a cabin on a cargo ship.

She had noticed it from the beginning.

'For me the only ills you'll ever have will come from the water. Don't expect them from me or from my poor wife, who can't even kill a fly. Only from the water, even from rivers. Beware of the wake of ships. Beware, above all, of the ships.'

Sweet old Jimmy!

And while he waits at that hotel in the shape of a ship, when he manages to forget Boris, the unknown sailor of Ufa, he thinks

about a stranded ship,

about a crack that opens wider and wider on the side of the ship,

about two large cracks, which expand like two jagged scars on his bare torso.

And around that ship that collapses, a baleful landscape: reefs, keys, sea urchins.

The sinking of the Titanic*!*

There's no way the ship can be saved now. Like a ghost wandering the long corridors of that creaking factory of iron he watches as it plunges toward the bottom. The entire story must revolve around the crisis of the female character. The name of Josefina is as arbitrary as the names of the others. The only reason he chose it is that it starts with J. Josefina, Javier, Jimmy. Boris is something else, the absurd, contaminating element: leprosy."

Then came the problem of situating the characters. The first temptation was to begin with the scene in which Javier tells his friend about the adventure with the sailor from Ufa. But such a beginning was unconvincing, a too-abrupt entrance into the material. Until, at last, he contemplates the scene with clarity. Josefina leaves the elevator of that hotel situated on the outskirts of the Tibidabo, in front of a roundabout with blooming carobs that, like lilacs and wisteria, are flowers that love winter. The hotel is an anchored ship, surrounded by a calm, dead sea, a smooth bay with an oily surface, whose waters can split the ship with the same disinterest as they would crack a hazelnut. And in its hull, Josefina longs to see Jim perish, not by water but cut to shreds by twisted irons, crushed by deformed hatches, rising and falling like sheets of tin paper. It's the first time in three days that she leaves her room. She doesn't even bother to go to reception to ask, as she has done with perfect idleness since the day of Jimmy's departure, if she has received a letter. She knows that in the event there is one, it will not be from him. She holds out no foolish hope (but at heart she still cherishes the possibility of those wonderful acts that confirm her vague belief in the unpredictability of human behavior). She thinks about her last conversation with Jimmy about the need for a separation, taking advantage of the trip to initiate his divorce in the small English town where he had married ten years ago. She heads straight for the hotel bar. She observes the waiter, who in turn watches her furtively. Whenever she wears that jacket she encounters the same looks, although this time it seems to her that there is something more, a kind of complicity that manifests itself in winks coming from the man who is serving her the glass of sherry. At the bar two boys look at her and whisper. Have they discovered her secret? Do they know that for the last few days, since the conversation with Javier and the night of the dream, she is no longer the same woman? How could she even think about a letter from Jimmy? It will be least fifteen days before the first letter arrives. She knows he will write to her without fail as soon as he's divorced. Deep down, he's also submissive, as submissive as the sailor from Ufa. Are all men of the sea? Are there many? "Your greatest enemy will be the sea . . ." Never-ending journeys, endless horizons, strange gleams in the looks of the young crewmen . . . Paradise? Limbo? . . . She knows what phrases she will read in that first letter, she knows the rhythm of his paragraphs as well as his handwriting. It will be as if she were hearing his voice when she reads once, twice, three times the short page. She'll keep it in the pages of the book she'll carry in her hands. What would she read at that moment? She must find an appropriate title to hide good Jimmy's letter within its covers. Broch's *The Sleepwalkers* perhaps? She would lock herself in the room and read it many times. She knows that she will make an effort at moral concentration and that after meditating cleanly and honestly—everything that Jimmy does instantly acquires an intolerable patina of purity—she will emit a definite yes. Yes, they would continue to live together: yes, he needed her; yes, he would marry her now that he was free from any commitment. But she already knew that, as well as the words with which he would express himself, because he had handled the entire situation, the hasty divorce, the brief separation that would allow them to think calmly, "without influence or pressure," about how convenient it would be to marry. She had taught him to yearn for marriage from the very beginning, on the very occasions when she extolled the advantages of an open relationship. And as in every romance novel, when the moment of the proposition arrives she would have to feign surprise, ask for time to reflect, and finally to pronounce a timid, a trembling yes, inspired by the sole purpose of making him happy. What a submissive idiotic sea lion! The letter would arrive in two weeks. As a matter of principle, as long as the divorce was not legalized, Jimmy would do nothing. But that no longer mattered. She had no illusions about receiving that letter, the letter she did not ask about when she went to the reception desk for fear of finding a note from Javier. She feared that Javier, in the face of her refusal to come to the phone—the hotel employees followed precise instructions: the lady had gone shopping, gone down into the city, she wouldn't return all day—, would have understood that she had gone too far and forced a meeting to clarify the situation.

And in Ibiza the rain continued.

"It's been like this for years," a waiter lamented. "Everything changed with the arrival of tourism. It never fails to rain at this time."

He lays out the various notebooks on the table. Concentrating on them allows him to escape the curiosity that his presence and his profession arouse in some members of that herd that has been forced into exasperating confinement. A Danish couple badgers him the entire time talking about the *Voyage à Kathmandu*. They're certain, having met him in Ibiza, that he's working on something about hippies and drugs, and they've decided to kindly assist him. The lady is more solicitous. She could tell you terrible things. About cases that occurred in Funen, the place of her birth, among people in her own circle.

Faced with the avalanche of their bad French, the notebook becomes a salvation.

He remembers that when still very confused he told Flora what had happened at Victoria's house, certain to impress her, she did not show the slightest surprise. On the contrary, what amazed her was his reaction. It was her opinion that the absurdity of all these stories lay in the fact that we still knew nothing about them, that certain taboos carried so much weight that they colored the considerations of the scientists themselves, which prevented us even in the present from being able to know anything about anything.

"One realizes that someone with whom he deals with a certain frequency, whom he sees normally perform his functions, corresponds to this or that category that he has always considered aberrant. Someone as nice, stimulating, or foolish as anyone else. For us it was normal until a coincidence, an indiscretion, or an oversight informed us of the alleged failure. Now," she concluded, "I laugh at such simplifications."

It was more than enough. A drastic remedy for the tumor. The great blow to the *pathos* with which he remembered the scene and with which he wanted to impregnate the story. This was, perhaps, due to the fact that the story remained in those notes for no other purpose, for the moment, than to free it from the *Voyage à Kathmandu* and from the cases that happened in the best families of Funen. How can one recover the insistent, imperative word, the silly laugh, the meeting in the dimly lit place, the image of the drunken sailor, sitting at the next table, whose hand cannot hold even the Coca-Cola that falls to the ground, just like, later, a bottle of beer and a glass? He hardly notices his existence. He gazes enthusiastically at a black woman who dances like a beautiful and graceful animal, sniffing a serpent; he sees her smell

the air and hold her arms out, with movements she imprints
only on her knees, her hips, and are repeated on her whole body,
are transmitted to her neck, which turns like an animal being
stalked, to her hands that clap in the void, to her nostrils that
contract and expand, until suddenly converting the rhythm of
the moment into a rumble of Yoruba drums. During a break, she
sits at his table, drinks from his glass, asks for another drink, and
tells him something he doesn't understand as the clumsy hands
of the sailor at the next table drop the bottle of beer on the floor;
she says that he does it on purpose so that someone will hit
him, but by that time the music changes rhythms and the black
woman gets back up and rushes to the dance floor. He's about
to leave when a group of acquaintances bursts into the establishment; they're looking for someone, Rosa explains to him, an
Italian photographer they lost and they were sure they'd find
there. They spread out at his table and the one next to his, and the
blond sailor suddenly becomes part of the group. The moment
Jordi suggests in a drunken voice that they go to Victoria's house
for one last drink, they turn on the lights in the hall, and the
sweaty clientele knows that the night has ended and, en masse,
they move toward the door; the sailor follows them, which seems
natural, because everyone is equally drunk and no one knows
that no one knows him. Jordi holds him by the arm because
he's almost fallen in the corridor twice, and he goes on to clarify that he's not his friend, that he's never seen him before, that
it would be better to leave him in a corner, the dock is right
there, that any other sailor, on his return, could accompany him
to his boat, but Victoria has taken him by the other arm and
observes that it would be important to see him react in a different

environment. (No, it wasn't that night, but several days later when she had a full idea of what had happened.) At Victoria's house, he barely noticed him. He heard him speak to Rosa, but he could hardly understand German, and the other one's gasping monologues were absurd, confused, suffocated by alcohol and sleep. The only thing he managed to understand was that his shoes were French, that he had bought them in Cherbourg, and they had cost him a lot of money, that his ship regularly made the trek from Hamburg to Barcelona, that he was born in Ufa, Bashkiria, which he pointed out on a map that Rosa took out of her bag, a spot in the USSR, north of Afghanistan, that in 1944, when he was only a year old, his parents crossed the border and settled in Germany, in Hannover, where he had always lived. He didn't speak Russian, he knew only a few words. His name was Boris. Then he narrowed his eyes; for a long time no one paid attention to him. Victoria herself seemed to forget her interest in the guy, and although, at that time, all he wanted was to return home, he continued to drink by inertia and also to hold whatever discussion by inertia, until he suddenly found himself seated again next to the character, who was trying to convince Rosa of something and, as if to show her the veracity of his words, lifted his shirt up to his neck. I didn't know what they were talking about. So he asked whether the two crudely healed wounds that ran in parallel lines from his shoulders to within a couple of centimeters above his nipples were the result of an accident or an operation; the other man replied with a guffaw somewhere between mocking and stupid and muttered a few words he did not understand. But, on the other hand, he understood the gesture perfectly; when he raised his right hand, he flexed his wrist several times, emitting a squeaking click with his mouth. He said a few incoherent words and fell asleep again. When the meeting broke up they could barely move him. Someone took his pulse, opined that he was too drunk, that it would be better to lay him on a couch. Victoria didn't allow it. They had to carry him, like dead weight, down to the street where they put him in a taxi and instructed the driver to take him to the port. It was daybreak. Rosa took him home. On the way the only thing they talked about was the possibility of an upcoming trip to Cadiz, where some friends were shooting a movie, and when he reached the bedroom, he fell into bed like a stone and slept until afternoon the next day.

He didn't remember the episode until several days later; he was translating an essay by De Sanctis on Manzoni; it was one of those times when work becomes mechanical and a word, a particular phrase, a certain cadence, anything, can serve as a mental trigger. It never ceases to amuse him the way in which the mind, free from vigilance and control, manages to recapture the most unexpected moments: a lost landscape in a lost sunrise, beside friends, alas!, forever lost, contemplated near Tlaxcala, the afternoon when he had a cup of coffee with a German professor and could hardly pay attention to the conversation, dazzled as he was by an excellent Kirchner hanging on the wall; Antonieta's troubled face when he told her that the tumor in her breast was cancerous, the sunset on a Sunday in last winter, when dying of cold he walked along the semicircular Arolas Street he likes so much, before closed shop windows, thinking that in one of those buildings must live the character of the novel he was then trying to write, the little man in the violet shirt, always frightened, and at that very moment, in the opposite direction, a drunken man approached, staggering, singing in a broken voice, Vicente Fernández's "*miedo, tengo miedo, mucho miedo*," and, suddenly, during that wave of memories that appears when he has already mentally translated a long phrase and his fingers move on the keyboard by an independent impulse, leaving a momentary cerebral gap, he saw the two scars traced on a milky chest, the two thick solferino pink edges that descend from his shoulders and stop at his nipples. She felt a shudder. His hands stopped on the typewriter. He saw again the living room in Victoria's house, his shirt sleeves rolled up, the two marks, the goofy laugh, defiant, complacent. And that image began to repeat itself, with minute variants, to obsess him, until to rid himself of it he decided to transform it into a story, and, suddenly, a more or less coherent plot appeared: the woman who's waiting in the hotel for the letter from her lover. The decorator who spent the night with a sailor from Ufa, the conversation with the protagonist, the nightmare, the further mental disarray. The third character, Javier, the decorator, has been friends with her for many years; forever. The friendship is very intimate: it was he who introduced her to Jimmy during an exhibition in Caracas. Jimmy could not resent that intimacy. Did Swann himself not entrust Odette's safekeeping to Charlus? Javier caused them to shudder when he recounted some experiences in the most beguiling corners of the port zone. Or caused them to die of laughter with his compilations of idiotic texts. But the day that Javier tells her about the experience he has lived (in the narration the experience would have to be complete), he creates in her an anguish that grows daily. That is why at first she's terrified to find a note from him at the hotel reception. There are times when his absence, more than Jimmy's, gives her an intolerable feeling of orphanhood. She could no longer tell him, for example, you're a real idiot, she couldn't tell him you're killing yourself, could no longer ask him what are you thinking, you're a barbarian, you have to bring me here more, you're destroying yourself, but what hours do you work? She would have to stop chastising him for so many things. My God, she could no longer say to him bring me here more often, I like it, I don't like these people, this place, could no longer ask him to tell Jimmy where he had been, because they often had to give Jimmy cleaned up versions; she could no longer ask him what he was talking about with that crowd, could no longer talk about the salacious topics that for them had acquired a quotidian, almost chaste tone, as if they were talking about the books they read; she could no longer tell you to fix her another gin, but don't drink anymore, you're going to end up in a bad way, you'll have problems, they won't extend your residency, don't you realize, you don't know who they are, or in what world they live?, where they sleep?, someday something's going happen to you, take me with you, whenever you want, I don't know what to think, you'll never have enough, yes too much energy wasted; no, please, don't tell me that, I'm waiting, I'm still waiting, I know I have no other possibility. She could no longer talk to him about her long, warm, pleasant, confident wait, could no longer say anything to him because any conversation would inevitably lead to that guy named Boris. They could no longer listen to records together, but rather they would only talk, whether they like it or not, about the blue-eyed sailor who threw glasses on the floor, hoping that someone would hit him.

One day she arrived to pick him up to eat in a small restaurant which they frequented with some regularity. They begin to talk about Ibsen. Javier is preparing the scenery for *The Lady from the Sea*; he's familiarizing himself with the time. He takes out a small notebook and shows her the gem he discovered the previous day in the prologue to the complete works. A defense by the prologist of Norwegian women so the reader will not confuse them with the perverse heroines of those dramas: "Let us add, for our part," he reads to her, "that not all have blue eyes. There are good and bad, conscious and irresponsible, and in this very variety lies their universality." And she laughs, delighted, thinking of the horror with which that prologist would consider the independence and rebelliousness of Scandinavian women. What if not a monster would Nora seem in the Spain of 1943? But Javier is nervous, he barely laughs, and when she asks what's the matter, he says that he just woke up, that he barely slept, that it's very hard to say what happened; no, he can't tell her about it, but he lowers his voice and describes his encounter in a bar, or better, in the street. (He would like the sailor, extremely drunk, to be found at the spot where Escudellers joins La Rambla, stunned to burst suddenly into so much light and space. Javier approaches her and asks her something, and just like that they return to Escudellers and go into a pub to continue drinking.)

"For a moment I came to believe that he was a vampire," he tells her. "I had the fright of my life. When he left I ran to the window and didn't see him leave. Either he was very fast, or he slid down the wall, or in reality he didn't exist. I sat in a chair and saw the coffee stain he had spilled, and, beside it, on the rug, an empty wallet. That reassured me. As terrible as it all had been, at least he was a person of flesh and blood and not a hallucination."

He begins to tell her very quietly, between pauses, the story. She asks several questions: he answers and, then, when they finish eating, they sense the void between them. Josefina knows that for the first time there are many things he doesn't dare to reveal; that, like Jimmy, she requires a censored version, "suitable for all audiences," or almost; he intuits that his performance was not as passive as he wants to make her believe, that he did not settle for listening to the sailor, that he has fallen into sufficient contradictions that indicate a more active participation in the act. But Javier will not be able to tell her what happened because he himself is very perplexed and tries to return to the subject of Ibsen, to his stage design, to talk about two lamps that he bought from an impoverished old woman who's letting go of her things, although nothing is able to create a normal climate of conversation and so, when after coffee, he proposes a walk, she raises whatever excuse; she has to wait for a phone call, then meet someone at the hotel, and he no longer insists; he knows it will be better not to see her for a few days.

After saying goodbye, Josefina will not return to the hotel, she'll walk without any concrete direction, she will seem to know the sailor, to have seen his scourged chest and will feel an enormous curiosity to know where Ufa is, Bashkiria; to know why he lives in Hannover, what his parents are like, what they do; she will imagine possible faces for Boris, will have the feeling that she'll never be able to feel safe with Javier; she cannot imagine or accept him in that role; she will seem to see him get out of bed in search of his pants lying with the rest of his clothes in a corner of the room, take off his belt, stand up again, raise his hand and hit him violently, she will seem to hear Boris' laugh and his plaintive voice that only knows how to say *schlagen*! She would want to kiss his wounds, to lick his scars, to bite him, bleed him, kiss him again, destroy him, and she discovers that what she doesn't forgive Javier for is having taken her place. Suddenly, she'll notice that she's far from her hotel, that it was crazy to walk so much and will take a taxi and for hours, in her room, she will savor the image over and over. That night she can't sleep, she tries to read, but she's unable to concentrate, she drinks a little cognac while she plays solitaire in bed; later she lies down again, thinks that she's becoming a ridiculous, fragile young woman. She remembers that Javier has told her truly terrifying personal accounts, one about the night, for example, that he slept with a guy who bled to death, and so many others. And then, strangely reassured, she falls asleep.

Her sleep is dense, suffocating, burning...

She's in the same room. It will remain a hotel room, but will acquire the look of a clinic, an operating room: in the bed she and the German sailor lie naked; well, a man who out of necessity is supposed to be the German sailor. When the man asks to be whipped she gets up and hits him with a black whip. She listens as he laughs with every stroke, like a grateful child; she begins to get excited as she unleashes the whip, although the pleasure is greater during the pauses, when the other man asks for more lashes, when he begs her to beat him with more energy. At that moment she notices that the man is speaking to her in English, and that she knows the voice perfectly; she also knows his back, the mole on the nape of his neck and, almost unable to breathe, she leans over him, raises the wisp of hair that is covering his face, and confirms that it is Jimmy, a sweaty, smiling Jimmy who, with imploring voice and eyes, begs her to beat him always harder.

For the three days following the dream, she has thought off and on about the scene. The initial feelings of surprise, horror, and rejection have yielded to another, much more violent one, of pleasure. Right now, in the hotel bar, while she thinks of the book she'll read in two weeks, in which she'll keep Jimmy's letter, she cannot help but think of his wide, perfectly golden back, splattered with freckles, covered with hair close to his neck, and hear the scourge of the whip, the voice of Jimmy who complains and implores, and feel in her fists the strength and pleasure she conveys. She smiles as a gust of heat invades her body, and it's possible that her smile reveals something truly wicked, as the two young men watching her out of the corner of their eye have looked away, now self-conscious.

"The sea is my enemy, my rival," is heard, without surprise, with very little emotion, as if the voice did not come entirely from her, "and I will be your friend, your enemy, when I'm your enemy, you will love me even more: you will be my sheep, and I will be your wolf; you will enjoy and I will enjoy seeing your scourged body bleed."

It would be the end of the story.

The holidays are about to end. Time seems to be hurrying. Now, however, he has to return to Barcelona. The time has come to board the *ship of fools* and to observe with melancholy, with envy, with irritation, that fauna to which it does not belong. All the notes, despite the corrections made, will remain for another project. Perhaps it is better to return to his previous idea, the subject of the little man in the purple velvet shirt who visits Barcelona, scared to death, with a woman who recognizes twenty-five years later a date hotel that she frequented in her youth, and with others he contemplates with sadness the Diagonal along which he paraded thirty years ago while muttering, beneath a fine rain, that his history has been very long, very sad; a cinematic story with too many episodes, but without a happy ending.

Barcelona, April 1970

TÍA CLARA'S DEVICES

for Anamarí Gomís

My first thought was to rip up Tía Clara's letter (isn't it absurd that I still call her Tía Clara instead of using the names she deserves, those I used once upon a time to refer to her, especially after she departed?), then, answer dryly, excusing myself. But I didn't do it. I knew, from the first moment, that on Sunday I would go to Cuernavaca and that I would continue to dance to the music she's always played; that I would arrive and greet her without too many hard feelings, that I'd then examine gleefully (it's one of the few petty revenges I allow myself) the ravages that the years have wrought on her. Yes, I will watch her wander about, feigning being lost, through a false labyrinth of imprecise and rambling sentences, amid retreats, omissions, apparent forgetfulness, only in the end to demand that I inquire about her trip, her visit to the country home where you now live, your health, aware of how wonderful it would be not to allow her to speak about anything but her ills, about the orthopedic corset that they've recommended she wear, the new method of lumbar massage, her financial problems, and her difficulties (feigned, of course, or, at least, terribly exaggerated) adapting to the country again. I would be happy if I were able to distance myself, to encourage her to drink all the cognac possible without allowing her, at least for a good while, to come close to the mansion on the outskirts of Tortosa where, despite all my efforts, I'm unable to imagine you. But in the same way I was unable to rip up her note and forget the invitation it brought, or to decline, or, at least, to postpone the meeting, to place her in an imprecise future, I know that neither will I have the courage or the strength, at a given moment, not to begin to interrogate her.

It would be foolish, worse, it would be false to say that my hand is trembling as I write these lines, as it did two years ago, when I scribbled the falsely optimistic notes I sent to you at the clinic, or, even later, the long letters in the style of *Anita de Montemar* or some other radio drama, which, like this one, were written not to reach their destination, but with the sole purpose of forcing me to try to understand what happened, to describe in exhausting detail each situation in order to examine it step by step, or, like today, having abandoned any attempt at understanding, to provide only an outlet to the exhausting strain that precedes the trip to Cuernavaca, and the awareness of news that will surely cause me to drink until I drown when I leave her house, and, amid the alcohol, recreate the demented gleam in her eyes, the subdued mouth of the woman who has spoken, and assume the petty rationalizations of that second-rate bureaucrat I've willingly become, in the face of the preposterousness of our role, yours, mine, in this comedy of errors dreamt by a mad demiurge, whose denouement has been so neutral, so dark, so tragic. But, does it make any sense to continue to go round and round on this issue? In the same day's mail in which she delivered her "plea" (the term, of course, is hers) there was an envelope with my photographs for the next directory. The doubly terrible moment possessed, at the same time, something beautiful, because the photos in a way confirmed a fait accompli. Your ills seemed at that moment scarcely a soft equivalence to the decay of features that, scarcely sympathetic, I contemplated in those photos. I discovered, without intending to do so, that I had found a way to be loyal to you, the only way in which I could accompany you, upon confirming my transformation into that pompous toad, full of trivial relationships, determined to scrape and claw for meager crumbs from the feast (that my name appear in the directory above that of the engineer Rocha, that the symphony tickets—I never go anymore, but I demand them anyway—be as good as those of the senior official!); upon demeaning any possibility of *grandeur*, of *gloire*, upon offending any future prediction that came down on us when we had scarcely begun university, by mocking, in short, the present of the promise that I was, I feel that somehow I am linked with your fortune. And that, as little as it may seem, is a comfort. Another would be, it comes to mind, as I reread the falsely supplicating invitation (oh, too certain!), to think that, in the end, Tía Clara's plan was not carried out, that a small piece of the machinery failed to work. But in the face of this you might have been able to laugh, to deny that there was bad faith on her part; you'd reduce the facts to an exaggerated romantic foolishness, like when we touched on (very in passing) the matter that time, the only time, I mentioned that by agreeing to meet at a café completely out of character for the kinds of places we then frequented or by keeping secret the visits we made to her home, we allowed her to manipulate us like a couple of marionettes. On that occasion you blandly compared her to the Henry James figures, eager for passions foretold in indigestible literature, such that for a few days it was Aunt Lavinia, Mrs. Wix, Miss Birdseye, names that did not catch on, because Tía Clara soon reasserted itself. I was not overly convinced of your reasons, perhaps because I realized that (you only came to notice it later) our friendship had begun to deteriorate, and that the deterioration had hastened thanks to her intervention, but I lacked the strength to assert myself, and then it was too late, I was as intoxicated as you, I needed her as an intermediary and as an engine of that something we witnessed, vaguely and indistinctly, and which made it difficult for us to be together in certain places, that made it difficult for us to sit side by side at the movies, that went on to create unbearable tensions like those from the afternoon when we spent several hours at her home, developing photos, half-naked because of the heat, barely able to speak, just a few days before that we took the gringas to the motel, where, I swear to you, my experience was no less terrible than yours. Those were days when we no longer spoke about anything other than our dreams and their possible interpretations (we almost dreamt them there; in her home), until you finally didn't return from one of them; and I, who was determined to watch her with the same fatal fascination that the lamb must feel before the tiger, saw her grow disturbed, furious, as if those lines were not written in the script, to the point of accusing you (she even did so the last time I saw her, quite inebriated, before leaving for Spain) of calculation, of voluntarily and deliberately feigning madness; that's why (I can tell you now, perhaps to justify my weakness upon admitting that next Sunday I will watch her drink snifter after snifter of brandy, cruelly and greedily curling her lips), if I continue to make these visits it's to verify—despite the many years that have passed—whether she continues to hold such a theory; that, even though I'm not able to know where the difference lies, it always produces for me a passing sense of relief. It's possible that I'm deceiving myself when I say that by writing these letters I'm trying to figure some things out. Well, of course, I'm trying to understand them, to understand why this had to happen to us —we'd long since passed the age of jerking off, which in itself could have been considered dangerous, without the slightest hitch—I try to understand, yes, but I notice that more often than not I take pleasure in exercises of self-pity: my attempt is nothing more than to revive and cherish the times of our adolescence, our conversations in the halls of university, our first girlfriends, rites of initiation: outings, rallies, assemblies, benders, poetry readings until dawn, everything that eventually remained on the margin, like a zone of degraded and insipid reality, when our visits to Tía Clara's became more frequent and we began to discover pieces of her past, of love stories, imagining nights in Barcelona, and glee-fully inventing for her an ignominious double life, unware that, at that precise moment, it was she who was creating a real double life for us: hence the sudden pregnancy facing our families, my inhibitions on the phone when your mother answered, and, above all, your grandfather, or, at my home, my sister; forsaking the usual cafés first to meet with her and later alone, when we no longer required her presence, in a horrendous establishment on Lucerna Street, during that period when our conversations had become strained and we did nothing but recount infinitely, one after another, our dreams, and search for all kinds of possible interpretations for them; but that exercise, while providing our relationship the necessary continuity, took place in the most remote depths of a forest of taboos; it seemed like an alibi, the pretext necessary to discuss precisely what we intended to avoid. We knew that the worst thing was silence. And I began to become distressed about your dreams, to invent other equally atrocious ones with which, in return, I attempted to astonish you, certain that yours were in large part false too, until that blessed Sunday when, as we left the soccer game, you told me that if we went on this way you'd have to visit a psychiatrist (you were so upset and shaking that I knew it was true), and I told you the dream about the pogrom (the only one I didn't make up), and my despair in the dream, and even after, upon awakening, and in the days that followed, at not knowing what I'd had done during the four hours that came up empty in the middle of the dream, and you foolishly believed that I was trying to allude to something else...Do you see? Do you see how absurd everything had become by then? We got into your car and went to eat at that restaurant that we both liked so much, the one in the garden at the Posada de San Ángel, where in the midst of a heavy silence I swallowed my dream and again felt her anguish, until, in an impulse that at the time seemed genius, you got up to invite the gringuitas at the next table to a drink, and as if by a miracle, we seemed to recover shades of the old days, the old phrases and smiles whose usefulness we knew perfectly seemed somehow natural, as if we had finally managed to free ourselves from some predicament, as if we had managed to escape...What hope! It was the last door, and, you knew, it led us into a trap. Sometimes I think it was like in one of those stories written by four or five hands, one of the authors introduced a certain register that only one of them could develop, a certain vibration, the parodic tone

of his own style, from which the victim, the one who's being par-
odied, is unable to escape, and although he decided beforehand
to write something different, upon seeing that text he couldn't
avoid the marked chord, and whether he wants to or not, he will
fatally write the story, or his part of the story, that the other has
assigned him. In short, it was a disaster! What a scene we treated
those good, docile, and unresisting girls from Alabama to! They
must still be wondering today what sort of maniacs they had
stumbled upon during their youthful trip to Mexico. I'll say it
again: the situation was also awkward for me. The best thing
would've been … (but can anyone speak now about what was
best or worst about then? We should've been more modest, not
thought in terms of good or bad, but rather what was possible …),
the only possible thing would've been to rent a room with two
beds, pick up the girls, penetrate them, to use each other's rhythm
for encouragement. But at a certain moment, long before that
day, long before you mentioned the opportunity of visiting a specialist, there was already evidence of trouble … There were more
than a few signs that heralded the total meltdown. Would you
believe that I never cared to know what really happened? My
only act of resistance against Tía Clara was to assume she knew
everything, and thereby prevent her from telling the version she
decreed (yours, precisely); the last thing I saw of you were your
frightened eyes, when I walked with my partner by the door in
whose lock you had already begun to turn the key, and then, not
long after, I heard the knocking on mine, and I saw the manager's
angry expression and that of the establishment's bodyguard, and
I heard the hysterical cries of the girl whom you had terrified,
then abandoned, and I had to pay a huge bribe to keep her from

going with those poor girls to a police station, and I rushed to your grandfather's house, where they almost kicked me out, I looked for you unsuccessfully at Tía Clara's house, in the usual cafés (it never occurred to me, to this day I can't explain why, to go to the café on Lucerna Street), until she finally phoned me, because out of all the people in the world it had to be Tía Clara you sought out (which encourages my suspicion that she may be right when she talks about a feigned illness). She told me that from the moment she saw you come in and avoid her gaze, she knew something decisive had happened; but I refused to know the rest (I never heard it); it was enough to know that someone had seen you, that you were alive, and so I did what I could to end the conversation, I packed a suitcase and left for Acapulco. When I returned you had already been admitted, protected from my visits by your family, your nurses, your doctor, so Tía Clara remained the only bridge between us; then I learned of your trip, the increasingly divergent stories about your illness, the acceptance of the impossibility of a full recovery, the wilderness. My life during these years, neither bad nor good, simply different from whatever anyone might think, can be summed up in a marriage that I could not walk away from, because it was ridiculously hasty, in a parade of faces (the last one splendid, although perhaps a little too stupid), in the transfer from one ministerial office to the next, in photos for the directory, in visits to Tía Clara ...

Of the two of us, it seems, you came out on top ...

Bristol, November 1971

CEMETERY OF THRUSHES

for Luis Deméneghi

The story he began writing on the ship and finished in Italy was not well received. Billie discouraged him immediately. It had no roots, she pontificated, everything in it was too abstract. It was impossible to locate where the action took place. Orión had other demands. Revealing to aspects of the world that the world did not know a cultivated audience. A few days earlier, he added, they had brought him the translation of an Icelandic story. Cleared of localisms and folklore and without the need for special glossaries, the author had elaborated a modern drama in which any of those present could be the protagonist, but at the same time it left a taste of the sea different from any other taste of the sea. It was possible to imagine a light that only the Norse were capable of savoring, a herring with a taste different from usual, without his (that boy with the straw-colored hair who regularly attended meetings and barely spoke and drank immoderately and silently) mentioning at all that light and those flavors; everything was implicit in an intimate narrative that happened in an apartment possibly like the one where the conversation was taking place.

She ended up agreeing with him, because in his story the protagonist should live abroad, in New York to be more precise, host a party to celebrate the exhibition of an old Mexican friend who's become a famous painter, and at the same time welcome his son whom he had not seen in a long time. In order to introduce the conflict that he was interested in developing, it was necessary that they live in different countries and that mother and son had barely spoken in the previous years. He barely knew New York, he had a mere tourist's vision of the city, he had never spent more than ten days in a row there, and so it was difficult for him to succeed in having the mother, son, and other incidental characters move about with ease. Following Billie's advice would have meant redoing the text altogether, which he was not at all anxious to do. If he had too much of anything during that enviable time it was stories. He had notebooks full of notes, sketches, projects more or less developed. Perhaps the ups and downs of travel always have that effect on him. During those days in Rome, he's unable to think of new topics, but he does manage to find attractive solutions to those stories he's left half-finished.

A dream was crucial for getting the mechanisms of creation going. He must have had it one night not long after his father's death, when he tried to forget that he had not accompanied his mother at that decisive moment, and dreams afflicted them unrelentingly.

He remembers that he wrote the story as if in a fever, inside a café devoid of any charm where he listened to the showers of autumn fall; it was very close to his apartment, a rather seedy café where in the evenings a young clientele met to listen to a jukebox. A place located almost at the corner of Via Vittoria and Via del Corso, the quintessence of a certain hardened and unwashed Roma. The only thing that resembled this Mexican people into which he had suddenly plunged himself was the rainstorms.

In his dreams there's barely any action; sometimes he has the impression that he's dreaming in slow motion, so static are the scenes. Someone begins to speak, and although afterward he only remembers a sentence or a few words, he's left with the impression that the person spoke for hours. Meetings never end. Just a few days ago, for example, his new pants, the ones belonging to the blue suit that Leonor made him buy a few days after arriving in Rome, had a hole in the knee; when he awoke he felt as if he had spent an infinite amount of time staring in amazement at the damage to the cashmere. Any dream can border on a nightmare because of such unusual duration. He finds it exasperating that it never ends, which can turn the most idyllic situation into veritable torture.

On the other hand, that sleep to which he partially attributes the birth of the story was full of movement and contrasts. He dreamt that he was a boy and that he lived in the countryside in a house with big tile roofs, a series of spacious rooms in a row that surround an interior patio, sunny corridors with pots of ferns and geraniums. The big house, where he lives with servants and ranch hands, shows neglect and disuse. From time to time an old man appears: his grandfather. From a certain moment on, he begins to appear, in a bizarre and caricaturesque fashion, dressed as a millionaire. He boasts a frock coat, a hat with a gray pearl crown, spats, a tie clip on his tie, and gray gloves, attire that contrasts sharply with the house's somber and natural deterioration. His grandson rejoices at the apparitions and transformations of his grandfather and the ever-increasing opulence of his attire. Suddenly the action suffers a twist. The house disappears and in its place appears a beautiful palace located in the residential area

of a European capital, possibly Paris. Don Panchito, an old servant of the house, his friend and confidant, is traveling with the
boy. Sometimes the palace is visited, which never ceases to surprise him, by Vicente Valverde (in real life Valverde was a former
co-worker, a guy whose capacity for intrigue allowed him to
create in a few weeks such mistrust and discomfort among the
office staff that, if he were indeed a policeman, as it was rumored,
it must have been easy for him to obtain any information he
needed: everybody was tracking everyone. The climate of abjec-
tion in which he was dabbling was such that when Carlos suggested he occupy a rather mediocre post in Education he didn't
hesitate a moment in accepting it). In the dream, Valverde almost
always visited in the absence of his grandfather and interrogated
the servants. Sometimes he saw him jot down in a notebook the
names of those who had sent the correspondence that had accumulated on a table in the office. The boy instinctively knows that
he must distrust him, and so he's extremely reserved in his presence. Sometimes he goes for a ride with his faithful Don Panchito
in one of his grandfather's cars, an imposing Rolls-Royce. He
can't help but say that he's intrigued by the origin of the fortune they enjoy. The money his grandfather spends by the fistfuls
can't be legitimate. He reminds him of the modesty with which
they originally lived in the countryside, the economic problems
of the old man, the hard time he had paying even the most elementary bills. Or perhaps had his life not been like that before he
appeared in a frock coat and a top hat? He hadn't won the lot-
tery, nor had he sold off any spectacularly successful business. The
only thing that could explain this bonanza ... and here is where
he revealed to Don Panchito his suspicions: it involved criminal

activities that, when he reconstructed the dream the following day, he was symptomatically unable to specify. He remembers that he had scarcely manifested his suspicions when the hypocrite Valverde, hidden behind the seatback, got up, opened the door, and, once in possession of the secret, jumped from the car still in motion. A few days later, the grandfather appeared very startled, with his wardrobe costume ill-buttoned over his voluminous body, and gave orders to start packing the most valuable items. Him he sent in the Rolls-Royce to a mechanic's workshop where it was immediately dismantled and converted into a very poor car of an outdated model. From the mechanics' conversations he learned that, just as he suspected, the grandfather's activities concealed a vast criminal organization. This does not frighten him as much as having to admit that because of him, for having spoken in front of a snitch, they were after his grandfather. Suddenly, looking out from the window of the dump they've fashioned for him as a bedroom, he discovers that the mechanic shop is located on the outskirts of the sugar mill where he spent his childhood vacations.

The recurring and incomprehensible presence of the mill did not cease to amaze him, as much as when he tried to remember his father as in the dream.

The afternoon following the dream he spent making notes about those distant holidays in the place where he went out every morning to have breakfast and read the newspaper, a café, as he has said, with bare walls entirely different from El Greco or the bar in the Albergo d'Inghilterra, devoid of the prestige of those other establishments, of their literary antecedents, of the concentrated atmospheres, and of that kind of opaque elegance that so often mixes with letters. In his (he doesn't even remember the name ... it no longer exists, he has been by there several times and it is now occupied by an antique shop ...) there was nothing to be seen outside of a stained calendar on the walls, or the three or four tables with metal legs and orange Bakelite surfaces, on one of which he began to enumerate the distinctive qualities of that remote tropical village of his childhood. That same afternoon he glimpsed the plot of his story.

He imagined a narrator sitting in a squalid little café in Rome, embarking on the reconquest of the spaces where he spent his childhood. A writer who at the same time imagines a child, his family, neighbors, and friends, and describes the moment when he first comes to know evil, or, rather, the moment he discovered his own weakness, his lack of resistance to evil.

By the time he had come out of the first trance he had filled several pages of his notebook with a tiny, secure handwriting, and had drunk so many coffees that he sensed that his facial muscles were about to take off. The noise from the jukebox had stopped, and a waiter, untying the strings of his long white apron, told him that it was time to close the establishment. He noticed that he had indeed spent some five hours shut up in the dive, that it had long since stopped raining, that he had not gone, like every other night, to Raúl's apartment, and that he now had a more or less clear idea of what he intended to write.

In a way it would be an investigation of the mechanisms of memory: their folds, their traps, their surprises. The protagonist would be his age. As a young boy, on the death of his grandfather, an agricultural engineer, the family had split up; his father's sister, married to the attorney for the business, had stayed to live in the mill. Her parents and her grandmother had settled in Mexico. Every year they spent Christmas together. He and his sister arrived with their grandmother much earlier and spent their entire vacation with their aunts and uncles. His early memories of the spot were very confusing. From this, he attempted to outline with the imprecision of a childish mind a story in which the narrator wanted to be a witness while at the same time knowing that he was an accomplice.

That protagonist, seated at a table in a café in Rome, would try first to establish, if only broadly, the obscure chronology of his trips to the mill. He's almost certain that he began to go before starting primary school; he must have spent his winter vacations there for six or seven years. But talking about winter and referring to that place was already in and of itself an insane notion, because the heat was a subject that aroused profound regrets, the cause of constant suffering for his grandmother, his mother, his aunt, the beginning and end of any conversation, it was always present, even amid the rain, and the burning soot that the tall chimney gave off accentuated it. Thousands of things are confusing to him; he doesn't know exactly during what trip this or that incident occurred. The conversations, the facts, all come together in a kind of unique time that sums up those December months of the many years during which he was and ceased to be a child. Above all because he long ago ceased to think of that time, he's buried it in his memory, he could almost say that he detests it, despite those vacations in the tropics, in any other time, having been the closest thing to paradise he could imagine. He sees himself with his almost white blond hair, in a short-sleeved shirt, short trousers, his legs full of scratches, scrapes on his knees and elbows, and a pair of heavy, frightening flat-toe miner's shoes. He sees himself running through orchards of orange trees, perfectly manicured gardens with growths of oleander, bougainvillea, jasmines, and poinsettia plants that separated the houses of the mill employees. A long wall surrounded the factory, as well as the house and the gardens that hugged them, as well as the recreational centers: the hotel for guests, the ladies' club located atop the restaurant, the tennis courts whose purpose was to separate that lavish oasis from the rest of the village. On the other side of the wall lived the workers, the peons, and the merchants: people of another color and another sort. The servants were one of the few bridges between the two worlds. Another, outings to the river; often a group of children and adolescents would go swimming in the pools of Atoyac to the curiosity of outsiders, who approached us to advise this or that way of swimming, of wading across the stream, or to point out the best places to practice diving. But the story was not going to be about the separation of these two human groups and their furtive contacts. The action would take place purely and exclusively inside, despite including the fat Valverde and the Chinese, children of the employees of the restaurant, who were treated like outsiders.

The protagonist thinks that if he revisited the mill he would perhaps discover that everything was much more modest than what was seen by his childhood eyes. He is certain that the garden was less spectacularly beautiful than the image preserved in his memory, that the houses were not as spacious, nor as modern as the series of artifacts, almost unknown at that time, indicated: stoves and electric bathroom heaters, for example. The foreign languages, especially the English he heard constantly, impressed on the place a stamp of foreignness, as most of the technicians were Americans.

He wrote down everything, everything his memory threw at him, without worrying about the quality of materials that this uncontrollable torrent offered him, knowing that from some of those apparently trivial anecdotes would be constructed a story whose germ he glimpsed when he recalled the dream in which, through recklessness, through carelessness, he betrayed his grandfather by revealing to his enemies the criminal nature of his enterprises.

He outlined, for example, *grosso modo*, a chronicle of the Mass in memory of his grandfather that ended with a quarrel between the bucolic village priest and his parishioners, who felt cheated by supposed anomalies in the collection to buy a bell, which freed him from attending Mass for the remainder of his vacation, as his family, which was greatly offended, ceased to attend the church. He wrote down more pleasant things, the bird hunts on which he sometimes accompanied his cousins, the frequent walks to nearby towns with an old mill watchman, an impenitent drunkard who would give them a taste of refreshments whose bottle he covered with a marble set in a metal ring that he turned with his fingers, refreshments to which he added a few drops of rum to give the indefatigable flock of ramblers the feeling of having reached the age of majority. He wrote of the fierce battles they had with the ingenious boys from the mill who had become "allies" and "Germans," where, inflamed by the rumors of imminent danger that were circulating, the first signs of which were the presence of German submarines near Veracruz and the declaration of war on the Axis powers, which none of them knew well what it meant, they felt themselves moving toward the spectacle of inhuman slaughters provided every week by the newsreels. He jotted down some typical conversations of the time, the monologues of his aunt's husband, the attorney for the business, seated at a table covered with beer bottles; violent and incoherent imprecations against his main enemy, the union, which he then extended to the government in general and to the local school in particular, the demagoguery of whose teachers, he said, made him want to vomit. And also the tremulous conversations of the ladies. Their nostalgia for the chestnuts without which no Christmas dinner would be complete, their horror at the news that stockings, and not just silk ones, would be taken off the market; Doña Charo, the enormous wife of the chief agronomist, declared at the top of her lungs that she would wrap her legs in bandages before going out exposed. The men talked of the increasing difficulties of getting tires and feared that the same would happen with gasoline. It seemed as if the elders had suddenly entered a world beset with apprehensions and uncertainties, while for the children the incentive of the risks yet to come made their games more exciting and wilder, and the hours allowed for their nocturnal exploits longer.

He wrote all this down, but from time to time he went back to touch up some paragraph or add new details about the Mass in memory of his grandfather, for example, ruined by the dispute between the priest and the parishioners. He was astonished at the importance in his recollections of the religious ceremony marred by a quarrel over the purchase of a bell. It was not the anecdote itself, the Mass concluding in such a turbulent fashion, he told himself, that interested him, rather the fact that there appeared in that ceremony the full cast of characters in the story that he intended to relate: he and his sister; the Chinese with whom he built cities out of bottle caps alongside small irrigation canals; the fat Valverde with his air of sanctimoniousness, his blank eyes, his hands clasped in front of his chest; the engineer Gallardo, that dry man with rough skin whom at home they called the lone wolf; his wife, who wanted nothing to do with anyone, their children, Felipe and José Luis, and their neighbors, who for years were their most faithful playmates. There, in a corner, at the entrance to the church, and even that a mere gesture of deference to her family, unaccustomed as she was to attending Mass, was Lorenza Compton, the girl who had changed so much since her father's death.

When he thinks of that time it seems that they were always next to the Gallardos. But suddenly he remembers that during the first two trips he made to the mill, the cottage next to his Aunt Emma's house was empty. He glimpses a gloomy house in disrepair with a minimal and neglected garden.

It is possible that all this is but a product of his imagination, that he's allowing himself to be influenced by events that happened later, and that these are the ones that color his recollection of the place. There is no doubt that in the last year (he had already entered high school and it was the last time the family met at his aunt's house to celebrate Christmas) the Gallardos no longer went to the mill. It is possible that the lugubrious image of an uninhabited cottage in the middle of a tangled garden belongs to the reality of the first vacation, when the Gallardos had not yet arrived at the mill.

He and his sister always arrived before the Gallardos; with classes scarcely having ended, their grandmother accompanied them to the mill, ahead of their parents, who would arrive much later. Like the Gallardos, who appeared on Christmas Eve, to, unlike their parents who only spent the holidays there, remain until the end of January. There were times when Felipe and José Luis didn't even spend Christmas at the mill. He remembers one memorable night, the first time they allowed him to drink wine at supper, when someone, perhaps his mother, looking out from the balcony and seeing the windows of the neighboring house illuminated, commented that they had been ungenerous, that they should have thought about the poor engineer. It was not fair that he should spend Christmas Eve alone, most assuredly drinking, naturally, what else could he do at that hour? His uncle commented that he had no reason to invite him; he would have responded curtly, he was the most antisocial man he had ever met, a real lone wolf. The comment must have been made well in advance of the story they intended to tell. That night, all the Compton siblings stopped by the house at the last minute, including Lorenza, who upon the death of her father, and for a short time, became very close to her aunts and uncles.

It occurs to the author in Rome, just as to his protagonist, to think of himself at times as a character divided by very different loyalties that do not make him feel completely at ease in the various worlds that he frequents, and who by giving apparently the sense that he moves in them like a fish in water has intermittently the certainty that yes, it is true, but that it is the wrong water, not that of the fish tank or the river in which he belongs. He realizes that at times his story tries to evade him before even allowing an approximation of the story he hopes to tell.

He has scarcely referred to Lorenza, the lone wolf, he has

said nothing yet of his wife, or of the Chinese or of the villain Valverde, apart from mere references in passing. What he is trying to say, in order to explain why his friendship with the Gallardos intensified, and hence the reflection on his ambivalent situation between Rome and his country, is that his child protagonist, through an indefinite and subterranean process, was becoming with each passing year a city boy who saw in the sugar mill an exotic and amusing place, entirely different from what the boys who lived there might conceive of it. Suddenly he saw himself as different from them, unaware of the keys that made the group of residents a closed, compact, and at times hostile group.

He eats a chopped egg sandwich, drinks his cappuccino, tries to understand what some good-for-nothings with indescribably filthy hair standing around the jukebox are telling two scraggy girls, who act very refined, emit a hollow laugh, move their hand, one to her coarse, wavy hair, the other to her worsted skirt, inconsistent with the stifling heat of that afternoon, as if she were trying to lower it to her knees, and he thinks about what began to distance him from his cousins and the other boys at the mill; of course his city demeanor, a certain way of seeing, of acting; different movements that came from Independencia Street, perhaps from the fact of knowing the escalators from the department stores, from spending more than half an hour on a bus whenever his parents went to visit Coyoacán or San Pedro de los Pinos; the tranquility of an existence spent indoors, while Alfredo, Huberth, Daniel, and also Mirna, Janny, and Mariana, sweaty and darkened by the sun, did not partake in that experience, and could instead spend an entire morning in a sugarcane cart, ride several miles on horseback, ride in the trucks that connected the mill's different outbuildings, talking with the stokers in an argot that was at times incomprehensible; it might well have been, but there were other things that made them different: the size of their houses, the spaciousness that neither he nor the Gallardos, packed into downtown apartments, knew, and also the fact that both their family as well as his lacked the foreignness that existed in the mill. But he does not intend to develop those lines in his story because he knows that it would lead him through other channels that are increasingly unrelated to the subject he intends to treat, and that instead, doing so would lend itself to long and inopportune interrogations from Billie, to meaningless discussions on the day he gave her the material if, after all, something came of it, and so he prefers to leave out all those affinities and discrepancies that little by little caused him to integrate himself into one group and distance himself from another, the one belonging to the insiders, that is, the one inside *stricto sensu*.

He could never be a travel writer in the classical sense of the word. It takes years to learn the configuration and to lay out the coordinates of a city; the simplest relationships between a building and a nearby plaza, between a monument and his own house located a few blocks away, are inaccessible to him. Describing that is almost impossible for him, it is work for which he was not born. In the case of the mill, for the effects of the outline he must do, he can think, no matter how grotesque the example may be, about the medieval map of a small burg that has grown in the shadow of a castle. The mill's immense factory and its outbuildings, the presses, the rum distillery, would be equivalent to the bulk of the castle; a park grew up around it, where there was the manager's house, the technicians, and trusted employees, the doctor, the lawyer, the administrators, the various engineers, the place of social activities, the tennis court, the hotel for visitors, the restaurant tended by the Chinese, etc., still more gardens, and other houses that reached the fences that would take the place of the ancient medieval wall. Two gates, perpetually guarded by a group of caretakers, granted access to the other world, that of the village. The houses of the insiders surrounded the ladies' club that served as the social axis of the place; everyone, at some time, large and small, found themselves in its purlieu. But behind the factory and the administrative offices, away from everything else, there was another miniature oasis, a woodland, a two-story house, belonging to his aunt and uncle, with a large garden and two cottages next door; in one lived the father of the Gallardos and in the other an old Italian couple that frequently visited his uncles. When Don Rafael wasn't talking about fertilizers and varieties of sugarcane, he talked about the situation on the European and Asian fronts which he seemed to know by heart. She, Doña Charo, an enormous and kind woman, spoke of capers. Well, about cooking, sauces, and marinades where the caper seemed to hold a place of prominence. From her distant childhood in Sicily came the caper cutting she was able to contemplate from her window, and in which, or so she said, she used to participate. He thinks, as he writes his notes, that with age the woman confused the caper plant with olive trees.

There is a moment when he feels that his narrator runs the risk of wallowing in trivialities for hours, in memories that contributed nothing to the development of the anecdote, and that did not in themselves create any meaning. That Don Rafael talked about fertilizer and Doña Charo how to grind heads of garlic with a small jar of capers and then spray the macaroni, who in the hell would care? Or that his older cousins, who were now going to high school in Córdoba and who when they spent their holidays at the mill, didn't stop at home except at lunchtime and sometimes dinner, that they went out early with their rackets, their rifles, and split their time on the tennis court, hunting in the countryside, at the river, or in the Comptons' house, where at night they listened to records, danced, drank rum, and caused the girls of the house or their friends to fall in love, all this made more sense because it brought the Comptons closer to the plot. These were a legion of brothers and sisters: their father had been an American administrator of the mill who died of a heart attack, leaving behind his children and a widow, a Mexican whom he had met in San Francisco who seemed not to speak either Spanish or English well, a woman whom one could easily mistake for mute, whom he often saw sitting in a rocking chair, infinitely fragile, delicate, with enormous dark circles under her eyes, wrapped in a shawl, rocking rhythmically for entire hours, without speaking, without looking anywhere, emitting from time to time deep sighs. Perhaps, if one thinks about it more, it was a case of mental weakness, a character that had not left childhood and who suffered from profound melancholy. She was the mother of a horde of perpetually boisterous sons and daughters, some of whom worked at the mill. Once the sons of Victor Compton, the eldest of the brothers, took him to their house and he was stunned. He's never seen a place like that again. He remembers an immense room where one could even ride a bicycle. There were bookshelves everywhere, not aligned along the walls as would have been normal, but in the middle of the room, dividing the space and sprouting everywhere from rooms where they didn't entirely fit; in the most unexpected places there were big pots with ferns and tropical plants, trunks, a drafting table where Huberth sometimes worked, and, if he remembers correctly, even beds. Someone was listening to a radio in a corner of that shed while at the other end a group crowded around a record player. People came in and out nonstop. Doña Rosario Compton, the mother, remained in a rocking chair with some newspapers and magazines at her feet; he never saw her read them; she sighed, rocked, very rarely called in a voice that was almost a whisper to a maid, to some of her daughters, to her grandchildren, and asked them to order cheese or refreshments, to order a lemon cake from the Chinese, to take the pots out to the terrace and water them. It seemed as though no one paid her much mind. She continued to rock, panting; if they did obey her, she didn't show signs of satisfaction either; she barely seemed to know what was going on around her. Hence his surprise when he heard not once but many times Lorenza, Edna, or any of the Comptons comment that their mother was always into everything. He never saw her outside the house, except in the garden, sitting in another rocking chair, sighing, moaning, with wide, owl-like eyes, accented by enormous dark circles whose blackness was possibly artificial: she asked the gardener in an inaudible voice to prune some plant, to cut the grass in some part of the garden that had turned into something worse than a wood, to lower the vines of the bougainvillea or the yellow allamanda and have them climb up the side of the stairs. Even when she announced her brief and monotone orders she seemed to barely open her mouth.

When he met them, Mr. Compton must still have been alive, but he doesn't remember what he looked like. Lorenza had just arrived from a school in the United States where she had spent a few years. Since her return she had become the life and soul of any gathering. She was not a pretty girl, she lacked the beauty of the other women in her house, she did not have, for example, that wicked air of a man-eating tropical orchid, of Edna, whom, after her divorce, everyone spoke of with horror; or Pearl's elegance; nor did she possess the natural attractiveness of youth that characterized her other sisters and sisters-in-law. Lorenza tended to obesity, her broad face of an awkward child was covered with freckles; her lips were large, thick, yet not at all sensual. She was, however, friendly and a chatterbox, her father's pet, and her brothers', and, perhaps, even Doña Rosario's, that is if she had a favorite. He liked to watch her ride on horseback like a lightning bolt in the direction of the gate that connected to the rest of the village. There was something crazy in her that was too uncontrollable, too provocatively opposite to the moaning stillness of her mother.

On one occasion she visited them in Mexico. Her father had died and she still hadn't recovered. She was a different, thin Lorenza, dressed in mourning, uneasy, who eagerly smoked one cigarette after another.

"I think I'll return to the sugar mill," she announced. "Not because my mother needs me, you know her, she's as strong as an oak tree. But I am convinced that in Mexico City there's nothing for me to do. I don't know how long I'll stay there; I think my brothers need me. Why couldn't I work in the office, even if it's translating or answering correspondence? Yes, don't look at me that way, if I stayed in Mexico, I assure you, I'd still look for a job."

They said that her plans were absurd, that she had grown old from smoking too much, that having lost weight so quickly didn't suit her. That December at the mill her aunts and uncles said that the shock had been brutal for the Comptons because it was so unexpected, especially for her, who was dependent on her father. Besides, as far as money was concerned, they weren't doing that well, such that Jenny and she were working. The best thing for Lorenza, they thought, would be to marry one of the single technicians who were arriving, or else she'd never settle down.

He had almost filled one notebook. The story was now clear, and he was able to glimpse the characters quite clearly. He still felt a visceral hatred for the fat Valverde. He found it repugnant that tragedies large and small could be triggered by riffraff of that stripe. The time came when the narrator began to order his materials.

Three possibilities were at his disposal to begin the story:

The first: A boy digs up a shoebox and contemplates how the birds buried a few days ago have become a fetid and whitish mass, because, to his stupor, notwithstanding having closed the box with adhesive tape, the worms had penetrated it and made prey of the thrushes hunted by his cousins. At a certain moment he notices a presence at his side; he sees brown thick-soled shoes and the bottom of trousers; he looks up and finds the sullen frown of the engineer Gallardo, who is observing with curiosity his grave-digger duties.

"I don't know how the worms got in." The boy explains the care he took in sealing the box so that the same thing that happened before didn't happen again, and yet the results were in view. "I buried a thrush under one of these rocks," he adds, a little self-conscious.

The engineer would say something that the boy wouldn't fully understand about the decomposition of matter: he would explain to him that even if the box were metal and had no cracks, any dead animal would become maggoty, because it was the body that contained the germs of putrefaction and not what was outside that introduced them.

"I would like for one of my children to study biology," he added. "I have two children who haven't arrived yet. They're coming to spend the holidays with me. They'll be here this very week. You'll be very good friends. But I'd prefer that you not play these games."

That was one of the possible beginnings. Next would follow the arrival of the Gallardos with their mother, the beginning and evolution of their friendship. From there the rest would take off.

Another beginning could emerge from the night during which, after the movie, Lorenza and Huberth, her younger brother, came over to have dinner with them. The whole family had gone to see *The Merry Widow* and returned in a great mood. Lorenza was radiant, imitating the widow's movements, humming the waltz, spinning with her brother around the room, letting go, sliding out onto the balcony, coming back in singing, having forgotten about her mourning, transformed once again into the merry girl from a year ago, except she was no longer the awkward little girl from before, rather a thin young woman, and, that night, even beautiful.

Somehow Lorenza devised a scheme to make everyone talk about their neighbors: the engineer and his family. Her brother commented on the unpleasant conversation he had had with the woman the day before. He and his sister were at the Gallardos' house at the time, browsing the books that the engineer had bought a few days before in Córdoba, and were studying in detail the illustrations of some volumes by Verne. They were able to hear the entire dialogue. He noticed how the Gallardos blushed with embarrassment, looked away, and concentrated on their books so as not to look at him or his sister, while the engineer's wife responded to a comment from her father about the film they were going to show the following night, threw the cards, one letter after another, on the table, and studied the possible sympathies and differences between them.

"We rarely go to the movies, and never to see those kinds of movies." She picked up some cards; formed a new deck with them, and began to shuffle it; then, while she went about dealing them, without taking her eyes from the table, she added: "From what I'm told, the atmosphere of the cinema is not at all encouraging, everything there is topsy-turvy."

"No, do not believe it," said her father, a little impatient now, no doubt regretting having begun the conversation. "Rubén Landa, the brother of the chief of the warehouses, organizes the showings and always reserves three or four rows of seats. One need not mix with the workers."

"I know that; I was referring specifically to those rows; that's where I imagine everything to be very upside-down…Three of spades!" She moved the cards from an entire row, arranged them in different places to make room for the three of spades. "There are people I don't interact with in Mexico City. I do not see why I would have to do it here." And with that she seemed to forget her interlocutor and concentrated on her game. Her father did not repeat the dialogue. He said only that he had seldom met a woman so unreasonable and ridiculous, that it was easy to see why the man's temper had soured. It was not surprising. Lorenza began to dance again, as if she didn't hear the conversation she had caused. It seemed that the widow's waltz would not leave her alone, that it had pierced her body feverishly.

The third possibility for a story beginning could develop the idea of a child who without being aware of the causes begins to distance himself from his cousins and former playmates, and when he begins to become friends with the Gallardos, a league is formed between strangers to the place, strengthened not only by their proximity and the fact that their houses are relatively isolated from the others, but also because they share an urban language, certain points of reference in common; perhaps because of a nuisance that he did not perceive on previous occasions in response to masters-of-the-world actions that the locals assumed; he began to find irritating, for example, their lack of curiosity about everything that would happen outside their domains. The separation gradually became more pronounced, not because the exchange of books by Verne and Jack London or the conversation about places in Mexico that only they knew gave them a feeling of cultural superiority. It was plain and simple a matter of a voluntary marginalization.

Their games consisted of opening small canals from the water intake that served to irrigate the garden and building on the edges complicated cities with bottle caps provided by the children of the Chinese or fatso Valverde, which they later divided into Axis cities and Allied cities and took turns bombing each other's fortresses, with fury toward those of the Axis and such benevolence and partiality toward the Allies that the latter almost always came out unharmed following the bombing. The need for bottle caps led them to admit to their games the children of the Chinese who tended the hotel and Vicente Valverde, who with his stupid smile and his infinite chatter never stopped repeating inanities to the point of making them ill. He seemed to have a fear of silence and a need to trample it always with endless and often incoherent stories. It was unimaginable that Valverde and the children of the Chinese played tennis, billiards, baseball with the insiders, stepped foot in one of their houses; however, perhaps because of the nature of their transit in the mill, it was normal that he, his sister, and the Gallardos shared their games with them.

One year the Gallardos were delayed. It was the time that they were tempted to invite the engineer to share the Christmas dinner at their house, when their uncle commented that he had no reason to, that he was a lone wolf and only managed to feel at ease when he was alone.

The irrigation had been suspended, and so for a few days they didn't make canals. In the afternoons they began to explore, always with the Chinese and the horrible fatso, a piece of land that was removed from the houses and the mill's social center, a creek located next to the administrative offices, where the manager's horses sometimes grazed, within the wall that separated them from the village of course. When the offices were closed there was not a soul in those places. They would go down to the hollow where the creek ran to pick wild tomatoes. He dreamt during those moments of performing exploits that would put him on the level of the children of Captain Grant or the little pirates of the *Halifax*, and he envied the adventurous life of the other boys at the mill.

Sometimes when they arrived they saw Lorenza leave her office. They watched her say goodbye to the others and follow a path that led to the rum factory. Hours later, as they emerged from the hollow, they found her back, sitting on a rock, with a rod in her hand, hitting the grass, trying to push a small pebble, or writing something on the ground (it's possible that he saw her only once or twice, but that was the most accurate image he had of her). Her expression was not one of happiness, but rather of concern, of absence, while the engineer Gallardo was walking around her in circles with large strides, and was speaking in a hushed voice, also with an absent air, equally worried and painful, without either one or the other seeming to notice the presence of the group of children leaving the ravine. He would not have noticed the exceptional nature of those gatherings had it not been because on every occasion the fat Valverde did not abstain from salacious comments.

At last the Gallardos arrived. They didn't go back to the creek. They began to play in the orange grove next to the tennis court where the gardeners had taken the irrigation hoses. By that time there were two distinct groups. The one with the locals, mainly athletes, captained by Victor Compton, junior, nephew of Lorenza, and the one with those who played bottle cap cities. And the latter began to receive increasingly more frequent signs of hostility from the former. Did they despise them for having accepted as peers people whom they hardly considered equals, or was it the fact of having devised more sedentary and less risky games that diminished them before the others? The truth was that they were no longer of the age for such children's pastimes. Indeed, several years had passed since the beginning of his friendship with the Gallardos, and he was about to begin high school.

Of the three possibilities, he found the second the most attractive to begin his story:

Pah-pa-rah ...

Lorenza continued to hum the waltz, she moved toward Don Rafael, her nephews, Huberth, circled him, gliding, moving close, moving away until she reached out her arms and her brother had to take her by the waist and begin to twirl her.

"Don't sing, don't dance! Above all, please don't go out on the balcony!" He wanted to shout at her, as he watched her distressingly put her happiness on display for everyone. He looked at his sister and found in her eyes the same look of fear that he directed at her that afternoon after talking to the mother of the Gallardos. "Stop singing! Come away from that balcony if you do not want your ruin!"

His plea seemed to have been heard. A moment later he saw Lorenza, her face shrunken, return to the room. A shot was heard not far from there, and immediately afterward another two. The first followed a confusing scuffle, a thick, mottled noise produced by the flapping and screeching of thousands of crazed birds that were abandoning the treetops of nearby trees. Lorenza was suddenly surrounded by a halo of thrushes that fluttered and squawked over her head and transformed her role as Widow into that of Queen of Night. An enormous bird, blinded by the light of a searchlight, slammed into a window, broke it, and fell bleeding at her feet. Frightened, Lorenza pushed it away with a sharp move of her foot. When she returned to the living room she fell into a chair and for the rest of the night barely spoke.

He was disgusted by gossip. That kind of permanent defense exercise with which the mediocre, the frustrated, and pigs try to cover up the lie that is their life, their intimate poverty. And at that moment, from the café in Rome, he's amused imagining Valverde as a child, with his moonlike face, his enormous ass, his parrotlike chatter, his eyes that seemed to focus on something with that expression that the bad guys adopt in the movies when they're feigning an intense look, his tendency toward obesity that made his shirts appear to be always on the verge of exploding, and his enormous capacity for gossip, which he accumulated and could unleash on everyone who worked at the mill, especially the wives, relatives, and servants, and the astonishment that his revelations provided him, his sister, the Gallardos, with whom, somewhat out of inertia, he did not dare to end their relationship, and also because of the need for bottle caps that he lugged around in large bags. In a certain sense Valverde caused them to lose a kind of virginity by introducing them to numerous personal hells, by considering them as something quite natural. But at the same time curiosity led him to deal with him, he sensed something repugnant in him; he imagined with great difficulty the hoi polloi in which such a creature flourished, the resentment of his parents, owners of the most important store in the town, for not having been invited to any of the celebrations that took place in the club or in the houses that lay on the other side of the fence marking the place that corresponded to everyone in the mill.

Once the character was drawn, delighted by that bit of snobbery with which he condemns him, the author opens the notebook again and recreates the day after the arrival of the Gallardos during which they had moved the space where they played their games to the orange grove between the tennis court and the factory, near where the other group that considered that terrain theirs met, and where, perhaps annoyed by the presence of that fat Goody Two-Shoes, they managed to deliver two or three painful blows with oranges during the course of the afternoon. That time the conversation centered mostly around Mexican affairs, school, the last time he had called (because by then they had spoken on the phone from time to time), movies, and books. The Chinese left, bored that everything that afternoon involved words, but Valverde remained until the end, trying occasionally to introduce into the conversation his comments about Sra. Rivas's greed, a Spaniard who had just arrived at the mill, or about Carmela, the manager's former cook, who had been fired and didn't leave of her own accord as she said, because it was suspected that she had stolen a pair of guinea hens; he claimed to know very well that it was not just a question of hens but of bottles of wine that she later sold to the foreman of the station, and in the end he commented that the Comptons lived beyond their means—it had been precisely Victor Compton who had thrown oranges at him that evening—that they didn't deserve to live in a stately house because they were employees of low rank, and the house was worthy of a manager, that they were so hard up for money that even Lorenza, despite her air of superiority, had been forced to work.

"Just like your mom. Doesn't she work in the store?" José Luis asked.

"Yes, but my mom doesn't mess with anyone," Valverde said contradicting himself; "my mom only uses the things my dad buys for her; my mom is married."

"What does that have to do with anything?" José Luis Gallardo insisted.

"Lorenza has lost all sense of shame. That's why she's become your dad's mistress," said the fat boy, pretending not to pay too much attention to his words. "He gave her a gold ring. During the evening, they were at the stables; we all saw. There wasn't an evening when they weren't there; who knows how long they were there, who knows where they spent the night."

Felipe, the youngest of the Gallardos, got up and punched him, first once then several times, while the fat boy waved his arms without knowing how to defend himself or even cover his face. He made one or two attempts to kick, but Felipe grabbed his foot, pulled it, and then started to kick him. They had to stop him because Valverde's mouth had begun to bleed. The fat boy left almost crawling; his sister burst into tears, and then, without transition, they began to talk about the Christmas that the Gallardos had spent with their grandparents in Pachuca and the gifts they had received. Felipe was short of breath, but everyone pretended not to notice it.

That same evening, the night before the New Year's Eve party, the day when they were to show *The Merry Widow*, when he and his sister were passing by the Gallardos' cottage, the mother called them; she undid the entire card game she had on the table and said, with apparent concentration, as she began to deal the cards again:

"So you finally got me to talk!" Her voice wanted to be gentle, but he remembers or imagines he remembers a repellent sound between metallic and unctuous that seemed to delight in the pronunciation of each syllable, in the utterance of each vowel; "I would like to know what exactly you told José Luis and Felipe about their father."

"We didn't say anything," his sister said immediately.

"My children have no secrets with me. Felipe told me everything. What did you say about my husband?"

He remembered the almost ancient conversation in the bird cemetery, when she and her children had not yet appeared.

"The engineer told me one day that the birds always have worms; that they carry worm eggs inside, and so do we; we'll all end up rotting even if we are buried in strong boxes. One day I talked about it with José Luis and Felipe."

"Don't be clever!" The woman shuffled the deck of cards again, her tone was terrifying, though the composure of her face didn't change, and the syllables were still intact, perfect, with each of the vowels in its place. "What did you tell my children about the woman you saw with their father?"

"We didn't say anything," his sister insisted. "Vicente Valverde always says really ugly things, that's why Felipe hit him."

"Really ugly things? Who is Vicente Valverde?"

"We didn't say anything," she insisted, a little desperate now, as if waiting for him to come to her defense. "His dad is owner of the store where the trucks stop. His mother is always at the store ..."

"He said that you saw them ..."

"We were going to a stream to eat tomatoes."

"And it was there that he met the girl? Who was it?"

"Yes, there," he said, and immediately felt the acceptance of the fact. He tried to soften his response, saying that it was the place where all those who worked in management went, so that it was almost necessary that he meet Lorenza there.

Upon hearing that name the woman threw her head back with a theatrical gesture. Everything about her seemed cruel to him, her powerfully marked bones, her mouth with protruding lips as if sculpted, her long neck. At last she concluded:

"I don't want my children to hear anything about this again. I will not even discuss our conversation with them. We won't talk of it again. Agreed?"

They left downcast, disgusted, humiliated, burdened with guilt, without saying anything. That night they didn't go out; they played dominos with Victor Compton, while they waited for the others to return from the movies.

Events unfolded rapidly. Everybody was surprised to see the wolf the following night with his she-wolf at the party given by the manager. It was the first time the couple attended a social event. She wore as usual a skirt and blouse, without a necklace, accessories, or shawls of any kind, with a face that looked freshly washed. He doesn't know whom they sat next to, whether they talked, whether they stayed together, since the children were placed at the end of the club. Upon remembering in Rome, the atmosphere now seems to have a radical strangeness: none of this apparently has anything to do with what he is, with what he has consciously been.

And then...

To the surprise of everyone, the married couple seemed to accept the order as if they finally understood their obligations to society. They were seen playing cards in various gatherings, he increasingly melancholy, she extremely talkative, so much that she seemed to have softened her tone, condescending to pronounce words less perfectly. Lorenza, on the other hand, vanished and for a season hardly appeared in public.

Did the others know what was happening? He tried to capture the conversations of the adults, without the slightest result. He asked one day with feigned curiosity whether Lorenza was ill since she was nowhere to be seen. The answer was quite natural: No, she wasn't ill, perhaps tired. It seemed that she was working too hard; perhaps her brothers didn't notice, or her mother, who was a despot, but the job was killing her.

One day (and he immediately perked up his ears), when he had finished eating, his grandmother commented:

"That man suffers terribly. I tell you that there are times when it looks like he's about to go mad." But the comment went no further.

How was it possible, he still did not understand, that no one was aware of the relationship between him and Lorenza if Valverde knew and his parents' store was a kind of local radio station? Was the world of the insiders and that of the outsiders so cut off from each other? Or was it that the insiders were determined to maintain customs, to protect marriage, to push aside the intruder despite the sympathies that she enjoyed and defend the rights of the legitimate woman, however odious?

Some three weeks after the party, the annual day in the country was held. They said that in the place where they were going, a spring near San Lorenzo, there were otters. A hunt would be organized. Don Rafael, the agronomist, commented on the day that the project was discussed that he had to inspect some cane fields in that area and would take advantage of the occasion to verify the state of the roads and the bridges and to make all the necessary arrangements. Engineer Gallardo offered to accompany him.

"He's very poorly informed about the goings-on in the world," Don Rafael said on his return. "He must not listen to the radio or read the newspapers. Who knows what his ideas are, but he doesn't believe the war is about to end. Not even the fact that France has fallen seems to convince him. Of course, I agree, one can't talk in depth with Americans, but between us it's different. Every time I asked him something, he came out with such nonsense that either he didn't hear me or he didn't know what we were talking about. You don't know how much he liked the countryside! He did nothing but study everything. I told him not to worry, that in the difficult parts, we'd carry the children. No, there is no need to be frightened, my men know the way well. Of course, one of the bridges is a little difficult, but I've already had the cables reinforced."

He can't be bothered to write the rest, to even think about it. Rather than put together the materials for a story and then weave them together, he takes pleasure in recalling insignificant details, for example, describing the large square wicker baskets that he hasn't seen since childhood, in which they carried the food. The movements of the day were unprecedented. The Gallardos were separated. He had to travel in the same car with Felipe, but they hardly spoke. He didn't know if he was aware of the interrogation his mother had subjected him to. He was furious; he couldn't understand how he could have repeated Valverde's words to her, but then, upon remembering how ill-informed the woman was, she must have been surprised by the conversation between her children.

He thought of making from that point on a list of facts as short as possible, without getting lost in reflections on external elements. The convoy of cars led them to a place where the cane fields ended and the ravines began, from where they had to continue on foot and cross two hanging bridges, a normal one above a wide and placid river, and another less reassuring one, a surely little-used bridge, a thick trunk placed over a very narrow abyss, but deep enough that it looked as if the bottom were barely visible: the only thing audible was the terrifying sound of the rapids as they hit the rocks. They rode astride the backs of the porters; there were lots of screams, lots of protests. The raucous voices and the confusion they produced gave the day in the country an air of total amusement. Some women gave up on the excursion, asked to return to the cars, although they were finally persuaded and crossed. The husbands, forced by the reaction of their wives, began to protest ... No one had warned them about the risks of the excursion ... Don Rafael insisted in a dry and defeated voice that there was no danger, they just had to be careful, that everyone had to be tied, that the trunk was very solid, he himself had changed the cable that they would hang on to.

While the others argued, all the children from the mill had already crossed, as had several young employees and technicians, the manager's daughters, the servants, the porters with the baskets and cartons of beer; someone put him on his shoulders and when he noticed he was already on the other side, sharing the excitement with his sister, with all the others who congratulated themselves for having taken the risk and emerged victorious, as they heard shouts warning them to stay away from the gorge, that there could be landslides. The screams blended into the violent sound of the water, deep in the background, when it hit the rocks.

They walked on, arrived at the springs. He had hoped to find the otters, the region's famous water dogs, to see them swim, to chase away their pups amid the invasion of their domain, perhaps even fight against them, but none appeared. They opened the bottles, laid out the tablecloths, set up a table for the cocktails. Doña Charo, who was charged with the preparation of the rice, talked about how the flavor could be improved with a bit of caper sauce. He burst out laughing because in his home the culinary fondness of their obese neighbor had become a reason for mockery; and she took him by the arm and in all seriousness told him:

"You must remember that a cat with gloves catches no mice," an expression that still intrigues him. Perhaps she was confusing him with some other boy for whom that phrase had some meaning, or meant that he had not yet undressed and was still in his underpants. His clothes, gloves? Perhaps. The others were already splashing in the river. Victor Compton, without wasting time, had climbed a tree and, from a branch about three meters above, to the admiration of everyone, performed one of his perfect dives.

He was surprised to see together, talking animatedly, perhaps with a certain false emphasis, Lorenza and the engineer. Yes, it was the first time he had seen them together since the arrival of the Gallardos. The engineer's right hand was bandaged with a handkerchief. "That cat won't catch mice," he thought.

They swam for a while; some went off in search of the caves that Don Rafael had announced. He tried to get close to Victor; but he had hit a shoulder on a branch hidden under the water and was stretched out supine on the ground, complaining and insulting everyone. Suddenly, Felipe asked about his mother and began to look for her. No one remembered when he last saw her, or with whom. It seemed to everyone that she had just been there. She had traveled in the Bowen car.

"When she got out of the car she got separated from us," John Bowen said. "My wife and I were sure that she had crossed the bridge and made the rest of the trip with her husband."

The engineer and Don Rafael went in search of her. When they returned the meal had come to an end, and some people had gone to sleep by the pool. Don Rafael had learned that the truck carrying the baskets and boxes had returned to San Lorenzo, but that it would soon come back.

"My wife might have returned in it. She's a bit nervous, but she doesn't like to show it. There's every chance that she returned without saying a word. In Paraje Nuevo it shouldn't have been difficult to find a way back to the mill. It's not nice that she didn't let us know. It's not her way. She's a nervous person, but such a thing is not usual for her, especially because it would worry the children."

And it was not until the next day that they discovered the truth. Had he sensed it already that day? Did his sister know? It's possible. At some point, they exchanged between them that self-conscious and accusing look that she discovered on the day of the interrogation, a look that she has seen in him several times since, as an adult, married, and that makes her think that he's hiding something from her, that she's afraid of him, of a verbal slip, of a betrayal.

The next day and those that followed were so extraordinary that even in front of them the adults spoke without the slightest care.

The body had been found. She had died from a broken neck. The current had dragged the body several hundred meters away and it had come to rest among some logs.

When did the fall occur? Who had seen her last? The conversations revolved around the couple's relationships. When had the wolf crossed the bridge? No one was sure. The testimonies were most contradictory. Yes, along the way the engineer had spoken to several people whom he hardly knew, as if he wished to make his presence known. His father also said that they had talked about some movies; the movies weren't as foreign to him as was thought, but his taste was most unpredictable.

The virtues of the deceased quickly began to be made known, her tidiness, her intelligence, her precision when speaking; of course, she was a bit eccentric, she had peculiarities, like spending the entire day playing cards. Naturally, there was something very strange, certain objects from her bag were found scattered on one side of the bridge; a comb, some coins, some cards from the deck, was it just a rumor or a true fact? It was difficult to know with precision.

He remembered his mother's comment when that was discussed.

"It must have been the seven of spades on the floor, which means death," she said, carried away by her fondness for melodramatic effects.

Everything was very confusing. An accident? What were those objects doing next to the bridge? Had she dropped her purse, and then, when she'd picked it up, had she fallen off the cliff, leaving some things on the ground? Don Rafael said he hadn't seen any of this when he got to the ravine with the engineer.

"Among the objects was the card that announced her death," his mother insisted.

"And the unexplained wound on the engineer's hand?" some people asked.

Strangely no one alluded to Lorenza. Was it possible that the encounters he had witnessed had only barely begun and as a result hadn't yet been noticed? Had they been so innocent that no one interpreted them like the cruel Valverde, save the dead woman, who could very well have been the victim of pathological fits of jealousy?

The following day some relatives of the Gallardos arrived to take them to Mexico City. The engineer, it was said, had to go to Atoyac to carry out certain legal formalities. No one showed any sympathy with his mourning. A shadow of suspicion stained the entire episode.

Shortly afterward certain irregularities in the work were attributed to him and he was fired.

He did not speak to his sister again of the conversation they had held with the alleged victim. Much less with their parents or their uncles. Once he was about to do so with his grandmother, because that secret weighed on him like a headstone. But when he had barely begun to speak, his sister intervened, abruptly changed the subject, as if to remind him that he had no right to be weak again.

The following year, when they went to the mill for the last time, in the cottage where the Gallardos lived they found living there a specialist in alcohols who was working in the rum factory, a young man, single, always surrounded by people; they listened to music until dawn, danced, drank, and argued, to the point of shouting. The exact opposite of the dying tone that had always characterized that house.

He didn't miss the Gallardos. Nor did he call them in Mexico. He once asked his aunt about them, and the only thing he learned was about the engineer's dismissal. During those vacations he had been very bored. The absence of his former allies did not improve relations with the locals. He played with them once, but he proved to be very clumsy at baseball. It was a failed attempt. Lorenza Compton was no longer living at the mill. At her home they sometimes said that she had gone to live in Mexico City, other times to the United States where the Comptons had relatives.

He finished the story; he rewrote it several times, emphasizing the esoteric aspect: the woman who read cards through which he perhaps learned of her death, the entirely casual circumstances, the burden of guilt. He established some relationships between the dream where he betrayed his grandfather and the confirmation to the woman about the relationship between the engineer and Lorenza. And one day, when he considered it properly finished, he showed it to Raúl.

Raúl thought that it was different from everything he had written, more linear, which perhaps meant that he was experiencing a change of style, that he was at last abandoning certain Faulknerian influences that had hardened him like scabs, and that the story could open the path that would lead him to find his true voice. He added that what he liked most was the description of the initial dream, the story of the child who unknowingly betrayed his grandfather, and that he thought that the oneiric theme was much more his style than the rest of the story. He alluded to a page in Pavese's diary that equated dreams with the return to infancy, since in literature both elements are but an attempt to evade environmental circumstances, that is, to deny reality. As a compliment that was somewhat doubtful. Billie's reaction could not but surprise him. She said the atmosphere was rather well achieved, that it reminded her of scenes from early Conrad, but she found the message laden with an atrocious nationalism, fraught with an unhealthy hatred of foreigners. How so? What do you mean how so? In the very fact that the mill, a symbol of evil, a kind of castle with a rarefied and ominous air, was an enclave of foreigners in the tropics.

An absurd discussion began in which she ended up, given the unrealistic nature of her views, defending positions that were irreconcilable to him; he made some concessions, attenuated this or that effect that could imply a condemnation of the means of the Comptons, and the story was published. Twenty years later he had it in his hands and he could show it to Leonor, who leafed through it for a few minutes, without being too much interested in reading it, praised the format, and then left it forgotten somewhere.

Yes, he thinks while revisiting that forgotten text, it was a bridge to other things; he began there to strip away the baroque effects that had long imprisoned him, which allowed him to move on to other forms, but only for a very brief time, unfortunately, since as he's said, for several years he hadn't written essays, articles, or papers. In any case, writing this story allowed him to free himself of his childhood, of the past, of the burden of not having gone to Xalapa for the burial of his father, to be cured once and for all of the illness that, according to him, was going to kill him. And, above all, free at last of his fear of Billie Upward.

Lviv, June 1980

MEPHISTO'S WALTZ

for Juan Villoro

When she opened her handbag in search of her creams, the blue silk pajamas that her sister Beatriz had bought for her in India and that were so comfortable, her slippers, and a bottle of sleeping pills, the magazine fell at her feet (she could have sworn she had put it in the black suitcase!), only to upset her again and render the possibility of rest even more doubtful. She thought again about the coincidence that, that very morning, when she tried for the hundredth time to persuade Beatriz of the damage to her marriage, not to mention her certainty that Guillermo was of the same opinion, and insisted that the truce had allowed them to know the sober pleasure of living apart, caused her brother-in-law to come to deliver the magazine in which "Mephisto's Waltz" appeared, which indirectly seemed to corroborate her arguments, the echo of which she had not been able to rid herself of all day.

She had planned not to read it again until she was properly settled into her home, after a bath, breakfast, and some rest. But how could she resist the temptation when the magazine had fallen back into her hands? So once she was settled into the berth, her hair brushed, swaddled in her cherished blue pajamas, the sedative taken, she read it again, and that second reading not only bothered her but caused her inordinate distress when, amid the repeated screeching of the wheels, she encountered Guillermo's voice again, its rhythm and diction, his gasping breath, managing even to perceive the pauses as he inhaled and exhaled the cigarette smoke. She read it without interruption; it was a very short text. A mixture of rage and spite began to take hold, insinuating to her that by clinging to those harsh feelings, she would be able to avoid the anguish. She repeated to herself that the natural thing would have been for her to receive this story, as usual, so that she could deliver it for publication; so far as she remembers, as long as they had known each other, even before getting married, when they were scarcely a pair of gay if not somewhat ghastly students in the Faculty of Philosophy, which she is so fond of recalling, he had not published anything she had not first read, commented on, and discussed with him. Yes, it was possible that in Vienna he had arrived at the same conclusions that she had tried to make her sister understand that morning, and that the publication of that "Waltz," without the slightest warning, was his way of announcing it to her. A challenge? Perhaps not, but rather a polite way of telling her that things were no longer the same between them.

All the grievances about which she had brooded at her sister's house (to which the latter did not seem to give the slightest importance) during the last week in Veracruz manifested themselves again. On second reading, the sense of danger was more acute. Something that existed in the background of the story, the final meditation on a series of small dramatic nuclei that were on the verge of crystallizing, of developing their own laws, of finally taking shape: minimal stories nurtured in the most rampant clichés of a *fin de siècle décadentisme*, hungry for gimcrack and tinsel (the shapely curves of a woman whose excesses lead to death, the ritual supply of poison, the criminal attraction of music, for example), yes, that meditation that, as a postface of an authentic drama espied by chance, was nothing more than the evidence of Guillermo's disinterest in the reality in which she was grounded, and made her think that in the conversations with Beatriz she had not known, or perhaps—and why not?—she hadn't wanted to dig too deep and therefore had been so easily refuted and deserving of charges of incoherence, capriciousness, and superficiality, for fear of confronting in earnest a situation that was almost impossible for her to explain. Perhaps her sister was right when she claimed that the only thing they had left behind was the age when starting the day, any day, could take on a playful character, an exceptional adventure, which she accepted as if it were the most natural thing in the world, but that Guillermo, on the other hand, refused to admit.

What she had found attractive in her husband fifteen years ago began to exasperate her such that, as the end of his sabbatical approached, she began to grow uneasy, to dread his return, to repeat to herself that the separation had been necessary because, in this way, she had discovered, painlessly and without worries, that the state of permanent exaltation in which he intended to live frightened and exhausted her, that he could not devote himself to his work with her by his side with the same passion solitude afforded him (the monograph on Agustín Lazo had taken him only half a year; she doesn't dare think of how long it would have taken him to prepare it with her at his side!), and, perhaps,— but at that moment the very idea makes her shudder!—the fact that in none of his letters had he alluded to that story meant that

Guillermo had long since arrived at the same conclusion and that they found themselves, not merely on the doorstep, as she believed, but well on their way to divorce. It was one thing to talk to her sister about that possibility; it was another to come face-to-face with the evidence. Her heart began to beat so erratically that she had to get up to take another sedative. Even from the other side of the ocean—which was truly indecent!—Guillermo was able to cause her such fits. For fifteen, seventeen, twenty years, the same thing had always happened: tacit but unreasonable demands, tensions whose cause could only be found in the realm of hypotheses, lingering depressions that filled her with a vague sense of guilt.

Guillermo was accustomed to dating everything he wrote. This is how she was able to know that the story had been written eight months ago, that is to say shortly after settling in Vienna. He had not—of this she was very sure—ever written a line about it to her. She didn't even know that he had busied himself with anything other than his essay on Schnitzler, to which he often alluded. In one of his last letters he spoke enthusiastically of a story about Casanova; he insisted that when she read it, she would change her mind about the author (about whom, on the other hand, he scarcely knew anything) and she would stop reproaching him for not having chosen as his subject Hofmannsthal (of whose work, outside a few opera librettos, he was entirely ignorant, though, for all the erudite references it possessed—his collaboration with Strauss, essays by Broch, Curtius, and Mann—he did find it considerably more attractive).

What she is sure of is that he alluded in some letter to the concert that clearly serves as the story's foundation. She remembers it because he insisted that it was the same David Divers they had heard in Paris when he had ceased to be a prodigious teenager and become a great musician. Her memory captures not so much the boy's talent as his beauty.

There is in the story (she opens the magazine, looks for the paragraph to convince herself of its existence, and, once she confirms it, sighs contentedly) a passing reference to the concert they both attended in Paris after getting married, which verifies that her doldrums have been such that even this minute sign is enough for the moment to make her feel honored. The narrator (because Guillermo creates a distance between himself and his narrative, through the narrator, Mexican like him, and also like him a resident for a brief period in Vienna) refers to the concert in which he first heard the pianist and remembers that, at the moment he stood to express gratitude for the applause, his wife—yes, she who is lying in the berth of a railroad car, is traveling from Veracruz to Mexico, and is reading a literary magazine—, upon seeing the pianist's temples bathed in sweat, commented (although at the moment she is reading, she is almost certain that she did not say such a thing) that the effect of those drops that were rolling down his temples and bathing his cheeks made her think of the face of a young faun that had just made love.

Once she had located the quotation, she began to reread the story from the beginning and was able to enjoy the beauty of certain phrases, to weave together the threads, to notice that the anecdote, as in almost everything he wrote, was a mere pretext to establish a web of associations and reflections that explained the meaning that for him made up the very act of narrating. In his first stories, the associations were freer, an outflow of images and events held together in general by a deep suture and whose connection the reader was not able to notice until the reading was well underway; in the later ones, the discourse zigzagged along a slower and more deliberate course, where the echo of certain German, and especially Austrian, authors about whom he had been enthusiastic since his student years was deliberately allowed to be felt. In recent times, he only wrote essays. Hence, too, her surprise at the appearance of this story.

Nothing Guillermo has ever written has left her satisfied after a first reading. There exists in her a need to play devil's advocate to her husband, to look for errors, to detect inconsistencies, to diagnose weak spots and fattiness in his prose. That is why he valued her as a reader. She, for example, would have blurred the figure of the Catalan woman who appears in one of the stories. She senses an excess of curves, roundness, an overly full figure that evokes for her hips like amphorae and breasts like the mascarons on excessively baroque buildings. There is an obsession with brocades, velvets, and lace, with "Veronesery," as she exclaimed once after having had enough, which always annoys her about his female characters, and which that day she perceives as a way to combat the challenge to her short hair, her small breasts, her narrow hips, her linear style of dress.

The story may not be memorable; her husband abandons it just when it begins to interest her the most. How does one compare, she says to herself, that set of assumptions that always border on the parodic to the real drama of the old man and the pianist, which he so arrogantly dismisses? The beginning was a kind of musical chronicle of the concert of a famous soloist in the main hall of the Vienna Conservatory. The first part of the program was composed of Sonata in B Minor and Liszt's *Mephisto Waltz*; the second half consisted exclusively of *Études* by Chopin. The narrator describes the sonata, for which Guillermo must have used the information from the program or extracted it from a popularizing book of music or a biography of Liszt, considering, as unbelievable as it may seem, his knowledge of that field was nonexistent, and he was never able to identify the simplest chord. Even though for years they may have gone regularly to concerts and apparently (which she doesn't merely imagine possible but rather is convinced it is in fact true) enjoyed them, neither attendance nor the pleasure it offers has been able to sharpen his ear at all. On one occasion, they heard Richter play Schumann's *Carnaval* in Rome thanks to a friend of her mother who was passing through the city, who, after moving heaven and earth, managed to get three tickets that cost their weight in gold but who at the last moment preferred to see the film of an artist whom she worshipped and to whom, according to her husband's secretary, she bore a striking resemblance. They went with Ignazio, and she remembers the occasion as one of the few during her marriage in which she could not contain herself when, with the glibness of an expert, Guillermo declared that Richter had definitely messed up the Schumann despite the ovation delivered by a multitude of ignorant bourgeois, that he had played it militarily, almost as if it were a march, that German Romanticism was very different, that it had infinite layers that the pianist hadn't even grasped, as she was still under the spell that the concert had cast on her, she let out a "please, Guillermo, stop talking such nonsense," which plunged him into a dark, resentful silence while they were at the Trattoria del Trastevere, where

Ignazio had taken them. It was an exceptional situation. As a rule, he waits for her to set the tone, to say the first words, those that contain the key, and then, with great coherence, and perhaps even brilliance, he elaborates a series of reflections on the subject. It amuses him when he enters his studio and finds her listening to a record; he's always quick to ask what it is, and if it is something that he would be embarrassed not to recognize (when in truth, if it's not the *Polonaise*, the *Emperor*, Mahler's First, or Beethoven's Fifth, he's usually lost) she answers in a casual tone, scarcely raising her eyes from the typewriter or the book in which she's buried at the moment: "César Franck's Symphony, of course!" or "the Mozart flute concerto you like so much!" and he feints concentrating until he recognizes this or that melodic phrase, which he mutters under his voice, then, satisfied, continues his task and even enjoys the music during those moments here and there when he is even aware of its presence. Upon remembering all this, as she reads what he has written about the structural complexity of the Sonata in B Minor, "so assailed at the time, repudiated even by Schumann himself, despite being, according to contemporaneous studies, the most extraordinary pianistic monument of his time," she becomes filled with bonhomie and with affection toward the man who isn't there.

The narrator, a young Mexican literato by the name of Manuel Torres, arrives at the soloist's concert, who, in the story, instead of Divers is named Gunther Prey. He has obtained, who knows by what means, a front-row seat, a short distance from the piano. The sparkle of the hall, the stiffness of the audience, their religious awe at the music all affect him, but above all the artist's attitude. The young man seems to have a blood, almost umbilical, relationship with the piano. At moments the exact relationship to his instrument and to the sounds he extracts from it makes him seem almost inhuman. Manuel Torres begins to write notes on the program's blank page, thinking that they may be of some use to him in the future. He has this habit. He has made notes on all kinds of papers, on restaurant menus, bills, on whatever piece of paper has fallen into his hands, only to invariably lose them in a few days, in a few hours, sometimes at the very moment he leaves the place where he has taken them. He jots down something about the pianist's remoteness, the magnetism he gives off, the sobriety of the gestures, the strength of his chin, the way his cheekbones descend then drown in his mouth before being reborn on tiny, cruel lips, which make one think of a greyhound, a greyhound with a touch of the feline, yes, a greyhound who was at the same time a cat from Egypt. She, who vaguely recalls the figure described, finds the drawing absurd and confusing, the usual trap into which men fall when they want to say that one of their male protagonists is beautiful. Blessed Tolstoy, she says to herself, recalling an argument with her brother-in-law, who, without any inhibition—and any suspicion—describes with joyful ease Vronsky's lips, his teeth, or his waist!

Suddenly something catches Torres's attention. It's possible that a furtive gesture from the pianist has directed his gaze toward a box located at the right side of the theater, just above the stage. At first glance the stage may seem empty, but if you look closely it's possible to discern a figure in the background, a man sitting in such a way that only four or five spectators from the first row, including him, notice his presence. It is a face that is vaguely familiar to him. His eyes follow the performance of the pianist as in a hypnotic trance. There is something tragic about the way the old man hears Prey play the *Mephisto Waltz*. At that moment, the pianist's presence all but vanishes for Torres. He begins to wonder about the magnetism with which the virtuoso's erratic hands attract those eyes, so fixed that they seem to wish to immobilize them. He notes in the program:

a) a military grandfather who attempts a reconciliation with his grandson;

b) a maestro about to die who tries to find in that concert a possible meaning to his life.

He imagines a solitary grandfather, a retired soldier who observes how his only descendant produces the magic that brings five hundred people together, by virtue of his hands, in an orbit on the margin of all possibility. He enthusiastically opposed his career and raised every kind of obstacle, including a violent quarrel that caused the young man to flee, which brought him more pain than the death of his children. With the fullness of time, he began to seek a reconciliation that everyone, he most of all, considered, until a few months ago, unachievable, a fact of which, at a certain moment during the performance, he becomes sorely aware. The young man's furtive look, the very one that Torres discovered, and which piqued his interest in the box, looks to be the beginning of a challenge. Every chord of the waltz is contemptuous, scornful, mocking. The old general realizes that there is no possible bridge, that he can never forgive his grandson, who offends everything that sustains him, for having descended into that world of minstrels, sorcerers, and clowns. There is a violent struggle of abstractions, which dissolve into the uniform he still wears to attend certain ceremonies, into the crosses that he pins to his chest with a trembling hand, into the massive sword that he contemplates at times with a veiled glance in opposition to those that flood his grandson's soul, which he flings in his face with ferocious virtuosity. Hence the boy's mocking and defiant expression and the old man's hostile but barbarously veiled frown. But for Torres this drama would become simply a story of a conflict between generations; he's ignorant of the workings of the military soul; he could never write from inside the story he has in mind; he'd become bogged down in unfamiliar terrain that would make it very difficult for his imagination to begin its march.

And if he were a teacher? A teacher about to succumb, ravaged by cancer, who with great difficulty has risen from the rickety bed where he lies moribund, to go to hear for the last time the pupil in whom he feels fulfilled, whose training removed him from everything that at a certain moment made him believe he was important: his personal career, fame, his other pupils, a wife, two nieces; and whose performance that night justifies his life and allows him to await peacefully a death that he knows to be inevitable and immediate. Although agnostic, in that instant, he beseeches the miracle of dying there, in the box, before hearing the last note of the *Mephisto*. He no longer wishes to confer with his disciple; what he desires least is to converse with him to ask why he accentuated the jeering tone that he sensed in his performance of the piece. He prefers to think that it is a sort of tribute, a consolation; a message that signals to him that, in the face of art, any personal drama is insignificant, that Liszt died, and his work continues, that he himself will die and then the virtuoso performer, but not before there are new notes that will surprise new ears; that love, misfortune, oblivion are mere words. But the tone of ridicule spills out, and in doing so awakens him (and then his astonishment is immense!) to the realization that nothing makes or has made sense, not even music, that his life has been nothing but a wretched joke, that the pain he suffers in his left side that renders breathing all but impossible is also part of that unholy joke, and he has a desire to abolish the world that in that instant is but a pair of hands that fly across the keyboard, mocking him, his dying, his left side, but also the music emanating from them and Liszt and whatever inspiration that may enliven man. He should like to stand and shout that everything and nothing is the same; above all, he should like to die in order to slice the dread of that moment. But Torres knows that taking that route would not get him very far.

Suddenly, he stumbles onto another possibility more suitable for the development of what has come to be called his style. He scribbles in the program:

> c) Barcelona, Palau de la Música. Effects of Art Nouveau; prolongation or, rather, revivification of an instant by way of music. He struggles ceaselessly to keep the memory of the story alive for a few days ... those that preceded (and culminated in) a crime.

The action would transpire in Barcelona, because it is a place he knows well, and although it doesn't require the exterior of the city at all, the parallel atmosphere of certain paintings, of a certain ornamental feeling, the ties between the Viennese Sezessionstil and Catalan Modernisme provide the tone of interiors required.

He can almost see the furniture in a spacious apartment, the lamps with lampshades of thick cretonnes, the pink stucco of the walls, the quality of the velvet of the curtains. A young biologist discovers after a few months of marriage that, beneath the placid and somewhat vacuous façade behind which his wife is hiding, a lava flows that reduces her to ash and delivers her to unspeakable practices under the tutelage of an Italian Don Juan. On one occasion, when returning from Figueras, where he spends several days a week doing research in his father's laboratories, he comes to know in a roundabout way certain details that lead him to discover the blaggardesque plot that has been staged at home. He knows that his wife, and this is what torments him, will never be able to love him, that their marriage has served her only as a cover to continue a life that was increasingly difficult in her parents' home. He decides to experiment on her with vegetable toxicant that he has received from Luzon, on whose properties he is working at the moment. The effect will be slow. He begins to administer the potion regularly; he watches her decline slowly, which reveals to him a fear that, of course, he feels, but for different reasons; he inquires about her health, takes her pulse at the most unexpected moments, recommends rest, that she spend several hours a day in bed, take some tranquilizers; he makes inquiries to his in-laws about past illnesses; he speaks to some colleagues, invites a well-known specialist to visit and examine her. The results are to be expected: the cardiologist recommends radical measures, one cannot say anything with absolute confidence, the clinical profile is extremely complicated, the only thing that could be said is that the symptoms are not at all encouraging, there is a marked cardiac decompensation.

She must be submitted to a strict treatment regimen. Anyone can see that the woman is expiring. During the afternoons, he rises, sits at the piano, and invariably plays *Mephisto's Waltz* which, he knows, in some way connects her to the lover whom she is no longer able to see, whom she will never see again. When death comes, no one even remotely suspects a crime; the young widower's pain is genuine, so much so that his relatives, concerned about his health, compel him to take an extended trip; he chooses, among all possible places, perhaps as an antidote, to spend a season in Luzon. For forty years or more, he has never missed the performance of the piece he is hearing now huddled in the penumbra of a solitary box. As the music floats around him, he still perceives the poisoned breath of his unfaithful beloved, he sees her bare arms beautifully shaped, her too-white flesh that descends from her neck and rises, maddening, transparent, opulent, onto her breasts; and on that occasion, in which Torres scrutinizes him with keen attention, he seems to perceive at times a performance that he believed long forgotten. This was how his wife interpreted the waltz, beginning with a somber languor, a great reluctance, only at some point to gain strength, causing the performer's individuality to be felt, and revealing an ambiguous background that caused him to realize that "she knew," that she was aware of everything, of the cause of her illness, but that in any case she was superior to him for the mere fact that she did not love him, for not even feigning to pretend, and that in the end she laughed because no matter what happened she had already lived the experience that was necessary to her and of which he would always be deprived, and in which he would never—not then, not now—catch up to her. And with every note he curses her again and curses life. He curses, in the most merciless and vulgar terms he can find, his cowardice for not having succumbed to the poison as well, for having survived her for years and years that have been a mere simulacrum. This is why the gaunt expression of the old man who contemplates the pianist receives a charge of sensuousness and another equally powerful one of hate. The erotic dose of the waltz seems to crystallize in the rigidity of the old man's face, more ominously still because of its tie to memories of something that once had to do with love. Manuel Torres, the narrator (and here Guillermo proves himself again to be a scholar), recalls that this piece, composed by Liszt during his stay in Weimar, is a commentary on the scene in which Faustus and Mephistopheles enter a tavern, and the violin of Mephistopheles hastens the villagers into a kind of amorous hysteria. Gunther Prey plays it at that moment with such intense perversity that the living corpse once again perceives around him the putrescent mixture of perfumes, medicines, and whiff of confinement emitted from the dying woman's room the last time she could still walk to the piano.

The ovation is immediate. The pianist leaps to his feet, his temples drenched with sweat. It is here that Torres points out that when he first heard him in Paris, his wife commented that his tense, soaked face made her think of a young faun who had just made love. At the moment when Prey stands in front of the audience and receives the applause, the electricity disappears from his muscles, the intensity is lost, his arrogance softens, and he almost seems to become a chorus dancer from some rather ambiguous nightclub. The writer raises his eyes once more and sees that the box that was for him the true stage that night is now empty.

During the intermission he discovers the old man in a corner of the vestibule, surrounded by a group of people who listen to him with an attitude of absolute fealty. A photographer approaches, a flash discharges; then the personage disappears furtively. Torres had time to ask an usheress who was watching the scene with delight who the individual was, and upon hearing the name, pronounced with unctuous devotion and not without certain contempt for his ignorance, he was surprised that he had not recognized it before. It's an eminent orchestra conductor whose photograph he has seen countless times in the press and on the cover of dozens of albums. It was he, he was told on that occasion in Paris, who discovered the pianist, who supported him vigorously in the international contest that launched him to fame. At the time, it was a matter of a boy of eighteen or nineteen and a man of fifty-something, a true master of the world in the fullness of his career. His despotism, his arbitrariness, his whims made him unpleasant to some, but these traits increased his popularity considerably. "These ruins you see," he mutters, and he immediately resents the appearance of such a cliché in his consciousness. The narrator mentally does the math; the pianist must be thirty or thirty-two years old, although he looked younger, and the old conductor, whom an accident that was never fully explained caused to retire from the podium, was nearing seventy, but looked to be much older.

The second half of the concert was about to begin. The narrator returns to his position, tries to pay attention only to the music, the box no longer interests him, the situation has been stripped of all pathos, it has become, despite the social prestige that surrounds the persons involved, their artistic importance, a mere private and suddenly anodyne affair. Reality has destroyed for him all the mystery possessed in the kind of dialogue that music established between the stage and the box. The eventual questions transform into an unbearable realism because he knows who the protagonists are and the possible relationship between them. Had the difference in age created infernos with no exit, delusions of possession, labyrinths of snares, and abject lies? he asks himself. And the accident in Morocco that the press spoke so much of, what was it really about? Everything now moves within the realm of hushed gossip and facile moralizing. Reality, apparently, so they say, is rich in low blows, not great deeds. The body, it is true, can make everything regrettable. Something shameful, embarrassing, the feeling of snooping through a keyhole prevents him from raising his head to contemplate the old man, and he finds Prey's Chopin boring, wrong, timid. Had he been in a less visible place, he would have left the hall.

She closes the magazine and turns off the light. She tries to sleep. She senses how much she must have disappointed him with the sense of reality she has wanted to impart on his life, and how old age no longer allows him to build the scaffolding necessary to live creatively. For her the most interesting part began at the point where her husband ended the story. She thinks that for the first time she understands why he writes so little, why he suffers from neurasthenia and depression. She thinks or believes she thinks about reality and almost feels dizzy. What is it? Is it in that compartment that her sister thought it a whim to reserve, since, according to her, she could travel with equal comfort in a simple berth, or in the lecture she has to review about the Suprematists, or in her dogs that wait for her and which she would like to bathe this week? Why, whatever it was, is it not satisfactory to him and, instead, has transformed him into a dry, surly, and bitter man? She hears high-flown words spinning in her brain as if trying to find an outlet or the proper connection, but the pill has already begun to produce its effects. She tries to recall a musical phrase by Liszt to no success. Weary, lost in a torpor that is not at all unpleasant, she gradually falls asleep.

Moscow, June 1979

BUKHARA NOCTURNE

for Margo Glantz

I.

We would tell her, for instance, that at nightfall the cawing and flutter of the crows drove travelers mad. To say that these birds flocked to the city by the thousands meant nothing. One had to see the branches of the tall eucalyptus trees, the leafy chestnuts on the verge of splitting, where the menacing clot of feathers, beaks, and scaly legs converged, to know the absurdity of reducing certain phenomena to numbers. Did it mean anything to say that a murder of thousands of crows or, better yet, hundreds of thousands of crows circled noisily under the Samarkand sky before coming to rest in their tree-lined parks and avenues? Not at all! One had to see the pitch-black throngs in order to stop counting the numbers and make way for the shapeless but perceptible notion of infinity.

"At the hour when the crows fall," Juan Manuel commented, "it's not uncommon for a Portuguese tourist to throw himself from a balcony on the eighth floor of the Hotel Tamerlane, or for a Scandinavian diplomat on excursion in the city to start cawing, to flap his arms and hop around in an attempt to take flight, until a medic comes and takes him where they will give him the necessary sedative injection."

"It's the crow's ferocious cawing," I continued, "at the moment of being ripped apart. It's there, at nightfall, where you see them fall from the trees, like rotting fruit, disemboweled birds, decapitated, their wings broken, pieces of legs, a cloud of feathers—quite the bloody spectacle, I can promise you!—while above, in the dense foliage, the frightened survivors hop from branch to branch or crouch down trying to camouflage themselves because they don't dare attempt to flee."

"Because a species of desert stork with long, narrow but powerfully serrated beaks," he said, "the *Ciconiidae dentiforma*, swoops down and tears them to pieces. I'm sure you know this, because, from what I've read, they fly all the way from the coasts of Libya and have taken over vast sections of Calabria. The most wretched cawing is caused by panic. Have you seen them attack? The Hungarian, Feri, almost went mad during his convalescence because of the din of these songful slaughters."

She looked crossly at us, and then, determined to participate in our conversation, declared glibly: "Actually, I believe it is the Lapland gull that feeds on the flesh of other birds."

"The Lapland gull? ...The *Larus argentatus laponensis*?" Juan Manuel asked with absolute seriousness. "To be honest, I've never heard of that species. Well, as you know, in matters of ornithology I'm a complete layman ... Are you sure it's called the Lapland gull? My reference books are rather elementary and don't mention it. I'll have to consult something more technical."

"The cry of crows sometimes resembles the weeping of a child; other times, most times, the cry of a hanging man."

Then we forgot about birds and without the slightest transition we began to ramble on about the sacred, mysterious, and opulent city of Samarkand. Its history, its architecture, its culture.

What mattered most was that she did not speak, that she be kept silent as long as possible.

"It has neither the charm nor cultural prestige of Bukhara," we admitted a few days before she began her trip. "Bukhara is the city of Avicenna, Samarkand of Tamerlane, and Genghis Khan. That's the difference, and it's enormous, don't you know?"

II.

I'm certain that when I was first in Warsaw my ignorance about Bukhara was absolute. I may have vaguely recognized its name in a novel. Is there perhaps a "Sorcerer of Bukhara" in *The Thousand and One Nights*? It's possible I had seen the name by mistake on the window of some carpet shop. But since the day Issa showed up with her travel brochures, Juan Manuel and I devoted ourselves, each in his own way, to tracking down all the information we had at our disposal on the Uzbek cities of Central Asia to put a stamp of verisimilitude on the stories.

Barely a few weeks ago, shortly before embarking on the trip there, I heard a Mexican theosophist passing through Moscow say that Bukhara was one of the navels of the Universe, one of the points (I think he mentioned seven) where land makes contact with heaven. I have no idea if it's true, but when I arrived in the city at twilight and glimpsed the concave configuration of the canopy of heaven, I began to feel as if I were in the very center of the planet. It's possible that, as I passed through the walls that surround the ancient city, the feeling of magnetization and magic it emitted, everything conspired to make it more powerful: I reached the souk, the casbah, the tangled backstreets of the Jewish quarter with the same utter amazement that my frequent encounters with certain books and films produced in me during childhood.

The heart of Bukhara seems to have not known a single change in the last eight centuries. I walked with Dolores and Kyrim through its labyrinth of alleyways that barely allow the passage of two people at a time. Narrow paths that unexpectedly open onto wide squares where the Po-i-Kalyan and Bolo-Khaouz mosques rise, the Samanid and the *Chashma-Ayub* mausoleums, the haunting minaret of Kalyan, the remains of the ancient bazaar. At a certain hour, late at night, the traveler wanders through deserted alleys (flanked by windowless houses of a single floor, or with exceptions two, whose wooden doors are adorned in elaborate carvings, each one different from the other because each narrates, in a way, the history and lineage of the family that inhabits it, reworked every 150 or two hundred years with the same borders, legends, and signs that they boasted in the eighteenth, fifteenth, or twelfth centuries) and hears, as if from another time, the echo of his own steps.

I gaze at the postcards I bought in Bukhara. What's certain is I don't fully recognize these places; I may or may not have been in them. It dazzles me, nonetheless, to know that I discovered the wonders that I shuffle before my eyes, like a skilled craftsman; I'm barely able to reproduce the city; above all I recall the noise of my footsteps, the conversations with Dolores and Kyrim, the air of drunkenness, of delight that came over me each time one of those narrow streets opened to give way to the soft forms of a mausoleum; I recall the music of Islam that floated through

some windows, and it, too, possibly little changed since the ancestors of the present inhabitants erected the religious center that
turned suddenly into a commercial emporium where caravans
converged from the different confines of Turkestan, and farther
still: from China, Byzantium, the incipient Rus, where they com-
municated in signs, uttered words that only a few understood,
and unfurled, among the arcades of the bazaar and in the adja-
cent places, their wares, exhibited money, knotted cords, bartered,
in a series of intricate market days, reeds filled with gold dust
and pieces of silver; where Toledan coins were mixed with those
minted in Crete, Constantinople, and those of the whole of the
Orient. After walking a night through Bukhara, the extravagance
of Samarkand, experienced the following day—so much gold,
so much splendor, such expansive walls, such high domes!—
looked to me like stuff of the nouveau riche, a strange delusion
of grandeur that prefigured a certain king of Hollywood. As if
Tamerlane had intuited the later existence of Griffith or DeMille
and delighted in showing them the way!

But not all was silent and still in the Bukhara night!

It was the beginning of November. The cotton harvest was
coming to an end in Uzbekistan and weddings were being
celebrated in its wealthy cities. There was a moment when
Bukhara sank into din and madness. And it was then, as I
watched one of the wedding processions, when I must have
felt the rustle, the first brush, without even being able to identify it, of a story that took place twenty years ago when Juan
Manuel and I were talking in Warsaw with an Italian painter,
a rather detestable woman, and we suggested she travel to
Samarkand. Now I realize that Bukhara had to be the city we

should recommend to her; everything then that we invented to encourage her seems possible to me in Bukhara. As we spoke to her about Samarkand everything we sketched out in our imagination was, in fact, the other city.

As we traversed alleys in our attempt to reach the city center, the true navel of the universe to which the theosophist surely was referring, Kyrim relished telling atrocious tales that he had heard at the home of his parents' friends, stories that in all likelihood were transmitted from generation to generation, and so will be passed on to the coming ages; they recount hair-raising crimes, cadavers dismembered in the most complicated fashion. The narrator's delight reveals that cruelty that possesses the desert tribes at the most unexpected moments; but like those of *The Thousand and One Nights*, the tales lack real blood, instead they are kinds of metaphors of fatality, of the fortunes and misfortunes that make up human destiny (for Allah will always be the Most Wise!) and instead of terrifying us, they create a sort of release, of repose.

It isn't difficult to imagine that when Issa, the Italian painter, made the trip to Central Asia she would discover Bukhara. It is possible that she contracted there the disease that robbed her of reason, the details of which we never fully managed to know.

III.

We told her stories whose extravagance more often than not exasperated her, although she did find some of them amusing. We made her forget her stupid sentimental conflicts with Roberto, the Venezuelan student who had had inexplicably become her lover. It was one thing to go to bed with him and another to take him everywhere, allow him to speak his foolishness, much less celebrate it. But if that wasn't absurd enough, it was even more so that Roberto responded to such passion. This neurotic woman, bitter and predatory, bore no resemblance to the young, round-faced blondes with whom he was regularly seen: the merry wait-resses of a brewery located not far from the Plac Konstytucji.

When Juan Manuel went to Warsaw we would meet to talk in the little café inside the Hotel Bristol. There was a moment, after having met the painter, in which we all but stopped going there; Issa drank too much, talked too much; the only thing she cared about was talking about her life, reliving her past glories (which we assumed to be false!) and at some point forcing us to listen to the countless string of complaints she harbored against Roberto, who promised to pick her up but almost always stood her up.

Before meeting her, on various occasions I had seen her dine at the Bristol restaurant. Always alone. With a forlorn air and at the same time one laden with disdain toward the world around her. I came to know by chance certain circumstances. She was a very rich woman. She was related to wealthy industrialists in northern Italy. She painted. Or rather she had painted in former times; she had exhibited in several important galleries in Europe (which had cost her a fortune). It was unclear what she was doing in Poland. Apparently, she had come in pursuit of a Varsovian lover; later she had remained in the country by inertia. Perhaps she feared return-ing to the bosom of the family and to her city weighed down with failures, hoping that her work would miraculously be recognized. One day I found her sitting with Roberto, whom I vaguely knew. The Venezuelan stood to greet me with a cordialness that I must have found suspicious. He took me to the table and introduced me to his friend. He announced that he had to leave for a few minutes and left us alone. We waited until the restaurant closed, but he did not return for her. From that moment, I could not get rid of her. She turned me against my will into her confidant, her audience. The tedium she caused me was unbearable.

She became overwrought with jealousy, alarmingly so. She cried in public, made scenes. One day she showed up in a less dismal mood than usual and announced to us that she was determined to cure herself of that love that gave her so little satisfaction. She believed that the best way was to put distance between them. No, she didn't think it was time to return to Italy; she was referring to traveling, to discovering new places, and that day, when passing by the offices of Wagons-Lits she was unable to contain herself. She had booked a ticket to join an excursion that was to tour Moscow, Kiev, and Leningrad. She arrived carrying tourist brochures. She would fly to Moscow in about three weeks. She explained that she had not been able to focus, that she had begun work on a large oil painting that could be her masterpiece, but that she had lost interest, the crampedness of her study was suffocating her; what's more, Roberto had gone to the mountains without even bothering to tell her, except at the last moment, and by telephone at that; in short, his boorishness had devastated her more than she could have imagined. When he returned, he would not find her in Warsaw; she would be on the steppe. The trip would help her recover the strength necessary to break it off with that heel and return to work with the rigor she claimed to be accustomed to.

Juan Manuel began to leaf through one of the tourist pamphlets, which outlined the itinerary that Issa had chosen and another that included several other cities, including Samarkand. A full-page color photo displayed the whole of Registan.

"How could you not choose this route?" he exclaimed, after reading a few paragraphs from the pamphlet. "For lack of money or curiosity? You may never have another opportunity to travel to those sites! Take a moment to think about it! Did you know that Samarkand was contemporaneous to Babylon? The only city of its time that remains inhabited to this day! Samarkand is a place where the most unusual things happen. Do you remember Feri, the Hungarian pianist who lived in Dziekanka last year? He spent the summer vacation with some of his colleagues who came from that region. When he returned he told us some mind-blowing things."

We began to use all the tricks at our disposal when we talk about such places, a hodgepodge of clichés, facile images, fuzzy details that confuse the Caucasus with Byzantium, Baghdad with Damascus, the Near East with the Far East, to talk about Yakut and Samoyed princes, barbarous rituals, and outrageous refinements set in Samarkand, and, as informant and protagonist, the young Feri, who had lived extraordinary experiences from the moment he got off the train and discovered that the friends who were to receive him, his old classmates from the Budapest Conservatory, were not on the platform; instead, he found two men with thick mustaches, one old, the other young, wearing astrakhan-collared capes, identical fur hats, and knee-high black leather boots, who seemed to study him closely as if they were trying to recognize him, to identify him. Feri thought that they might be relatives of his friends who for some unforeseen reason had come to welcome him in their place; Feri approached them and asked in a very rudimentary Russian if they had come for him; he explained that his name was Feri Nagy and provided the name of the young men who studied with him in Budapest. They answered yes in Russian; afterward they held a brief exchange among themselves in their language, which he found to be excessively formal. The younger man took the suitcase and with a ceremonious gesture invited him to follow.

"Feri said that they crossed the Asian city's threshold, a veritable souk of narrow alleyways, truncated walls, regally carved gates that overlooked inner courtyards populated with pomegranates, rosebushes, and hordes of children capable of producing a commotion almost as deafening as that of the crows that he later saw every dusk in the gardens of the city. The children peered out of the doors, fat and big-headed, making strange sounds in their language as if warning him to return, that there was still time to return to the station and catch the first train that would take him away from Samarkand. He said the sound resembled a phrase that in Hungarian means: 'Go back to your house, Satan!'"

One of us described the house they reached as different from the others. In a corner, a blind wall and a door; on a second floor, a tiny window protected by iron bars. They entered, crossed the courtyard, which was also planted with rosebushes and pomegranate trees, and different only from the rest by the absence of children. The old man and the young man in astrakhan-collared coats walked very erect, and with identical martialed movements climbed a narrow staircase leading to a terrace. They crossed that terrace to a very sparse, almost monastic room, the furniture of which consisted only of a narrow bed and a small table and washbasin. The old man clapped once or twice and launched a barrage of intemperate shouts that were out of keeping with the severity of his manners. A young girl appeared with a pitcher of water and filled the basin. Feri had always found it awkward to wash himself in the presence of others, but he had no choice but to take off his shirt and wash his face, neck, and arms in front of the two men, who, standing at the door of the room, had taken on a character of custodians rather than hosts. He took a shirt from his valise and was about to get dressed when the young woman returned with an Arab djellaba and at the old man's instructions, which bordered on orders, he had no choice but to put it on.

"He felt ridiculous. You knew Feri," Juan Manuel asked again, "didn't you? He was a very young boy, very timid, incapable of offering the slightest resistance. I can imagine him very well in that situation, obeying any order they gave without even questioning it. Besides, in what language could he answer? Every time he tried to say something in Russian, they answered yes, of course, certainly, but they kept talking to each other in that language in which he didn't understand a single word."

Then they went into the sitting room. A young man his age, dressed in European clothes, such that anyone would have confused him with a boy from Southern Europe, someone from Palermo or Athens, for example, welcomed him and showed him to a chair next to the princess.

"What princess?" the Italian asked at last, with a hint of interest. They had to explain to her that Feri had landed in a family of Circassian nobles.

"In Samarkand there can still be found descendants of some of the oldest families in the world."

They were seated on carpets among mounds of pillows and cushions. Everything in the room was elegant and at the same time very dirty. It was not an obvious elegance; it was difficult to detect, to know in what and where it resided. Only someone who had seen the outside world would notice it. An ordinary mortal would have found nothing but confusion, filth, and chaos. The old princess was covered in rich brocades, but was barefoot, and the stench that her body gave off was unspeakable: a mixture of sweat, dirty feet, clothes that had never been washed, rancid oils, and vulgar perfumes. The men, on the other hand, seemed very clean. The grandson was the only one in European dress; the others, women and men, were dressed in the most outlandish way imaginable; almost everyone wore black knee-length boots, some wore gold tunics, and others leather and suede jackets and trousers, with astrakhan caps and collars; the women wearing bloomers barely concealed by tunics in vivid colors. The effect, according to Feri, who was terribly unobservant, looked like the amplification of a Persian miniature.

"Does that tell you anything?" I interrupted, addressing Issa. "To be honest, nothing. A Persian miniature? What does that mean? Persian miniatures can illustrate all sorts of situations, from harems to hunting. The Hungarians, you know, are Asians; that's why our dear Feri Nagy had begun to feel like a fish in water. He didn't need words to communicate with them. He wasn't able to describe the gathering very well because for him there was nothing unusual about it. It was as natural for him as attending a birthday dinner at the Gellért in Budapest, except he didn't like the old woman, the princess, at all.

"But where had he gotten himself? The bazaar?"

"You haven't understood anything, because deep down you're just like Feri. It doesn't matter if they are here or there. They find everything natural. What do you mean were they in the bazaar? We've tried for hours to explain to you that it was a gathering at the home of Circassian princes!"

"To begin with, I'm sure there are no private houses or princes of any kind there. What I think is that all Feri has done is tell you a pack of lies and that you've believed them."

"It's possible. But I assure you he didn't invent the scars; we saw them."

"Yes, we did see them; and may I add they weren't a game. All right, let's take things in order: first, they began to pass around dishes, lamb stews, bunches of aromatic herbs, and at the same time, without any order at all, honey sweets, pine nuts, pistachios, spicy seeds, bowls of soups, and, to complement the food, peach brandy, which according to Feri was exquisite. Up until a certain moment, the old woman, despite being very close to him, was very distant; she treated him arrogantly and with contempt, like an interloper who had wheedled his way into her rooms using who knows what ruse. But by the second or third cup she began to smile at him, to say things to him he didn't understand, to give him candy with her pudgy fingers with nails of an obviously perpetual blackness. The boy dressed in European clothes did not eat: he sat in a corner and played a monotonous rhythm on a tiny drum and softly intoned a languorous oriental song; his face at times acquired an almost feminine expression. That food, the mixtures of fats and honey, would only have made me nauseous; Feri, on the other hand, was delighted. They all came over to him, surrounded him, smiled, poured him glass after glass of brandy, passed him lamb chops and sweets, fed him dates with their hands. What a handful that Feri! By now, he was perfectly accustomed to the stench that he found so offensive at first, and not only that, he breathed it in with delight, as if it were a complement to the honey of the sweets and the aroma of the brandy. Yes, at a given moment, he felt as if he had reached the Promised Land; he tried to stand to offer a toast but discovered that his legs would barely obey him. Feri's clumsiness is proverbial, and as a drinker, don't even ask, the worst. He hastily sat back down to conceal his deficiencies. The others, by then, were already piled around him, smiling, eagerly awaiting his words, his gestures. On all their faces, down their open collars, sweat ran profusely. Only one girl, the one who had brought the water and basin to his small bedroom, withdrew at that moment to another corner of the room and began to mumble under her breath a tune that was a counterpoint to that of her companion, the boy in European dress. The features of the pair of musicians were severe, absent, as if they were both in a trance, in comparison with the other members of the family, who burst out laughing only to become silent suddenly; there was no doubt that they were expecting something to happen; their eyes sparkled, their teeth gleamed. Feri had never seen teeth so white and shining in his life. Incapable, then, of standing up, he stuck out his chest, extended an arm, raised his cup and toasted, to the nightingales' song, to friendship, to the color of the pomegranate, to this evening's gathering. His voice, did you ever hear it? What a shame! It's hard to believe that you never met him! Feri was the king of Dziekanka; a boy with a beautifully melodic voice, a deep, nicely trained baritone voice. When he spoke in Hungarian it sounded like he was singing. Apparently these were the words the princes were waiting for. He had scarcely stopped talking when the drums resounded with a frenzy and the rest of the assembled guests unleashed a savage cry, though rather than savage a better adjective would be ancient; it was a prehistoric howl. A hand passed him another cup, without any doubt the old woman, who took advantage of the moment to let out a brazen laugh and stroke his cheek with her dirty, calloused hands. It was the last thing he remembered about that night. When he awoke he was naked in the narrow cot of the room where he had been taken when he arrived. He thought he was going to die. His body ached terribly; not everything, because there were parts, his legs, for example, that he couldn't feel at all. For a moment he was terrified that they had been amputated. He struggled to lower his arm to feel his thighs: they were there. He raised his head enough so he could see his whole body, stained as if someone had poured a bucket of tincture of pomegranate on it. It didn't take much effort to realize that the spots were in fact clumps of blood, hardened and blackish, that his body was horribly injured, that some of the wounds, which seemed to be several days old, were distinctly worrisome, most certainly had been inflicted several days before, and were on the verge of becoming infected. He sat up as best he could. He covered his body with a sheet. He was too weak to dress himself. He went downstairs, crossed the courtyard, deserted at that hour, and reached the street. It was dawn. He walked a few blocks. Lights came on in some windows. He heard footsteps close to him. He mustered all his remaining strength and cried out before falling unconscious. He awoke in the hospital; he couldn't tell if hours or days had passed since he fainted. His only amusement—if it could be called amusement!—as his wounds healed, which were not so serious despite their outward appearance, although those in his groin were indeed very painful, consisted of venturing out onto the balcony in the afternoon, watching the sunset, and observing the surprising arrival of the desert storks to launch their harvest of crows. When he was discharged, he searched desperately for the house where he had attended the banquet but failed to locate it. On several occasions he went to the train station at the time when the trains arrived in the hope that chance might reunite him with his hosts, but they never appeared. Feri is like that, completely Oriental: he had found his piece of heaven and didn't want to lose it. Finally, he was forced to leave the city and return to Warsaw. He now lived in another world. He refused to continue his studies. He spoke of elixirs, of pleasures that we would never understand, and since no one paid him any attention, he eventually returned to his country. He lost interest in the piano, they say, which is a shame because he was indeed a gifted boy."

"I have no doubt that this Feri has done nothing but have fun at your expense. He wouldn't have dared to tell me such a tissue of nonsense."

"Perhaps; you Europeans are better at navigating such things. Either way, no matter what the people are like, just seeing the monuments makes it worth it. Just think about the bazaars, the weaving! After all, it's about experiencing another continent!"

"Perhaps it's worth it."

And one day she announced that she had changed her ticket, that she was leaving in three or four days, and that she would tell us about her experiences in Samarkand when she returned. We never got to hear them.

IV.

Juan Manuel Torres once made me read a text by Jan Kott: "A Short Treatise on Eroticism." I look for it on my shelf of Polish literature and in the English edition I find the quote I was thinking of the day after our nocturnal tour of Bukhara, as we were preparing to fly to Samarkand. I recalled with Kyrim and Dolores the wedding ceremonies. It reads: "In darkness the body is split into fragments, into separate objects. They have an independent existence. It is my touch that makes them exist *for me*. Touch in a limited sense. Unlike sight, it doesn't embrace the entire person. Touch is invariably fragmentary; it decomposes. A body experienced through touch is never an entity; it is just a sum of fragments that exist side by side."

I had tried to remember that quotation as I left Bukhara, and when I read it, I was pleased to see that I hadn't gotten the meaning wrong. We were at the airport, in an outdoor waiting room. Under the vine arbor there was a series of small tables and wooden benches scattered in a large garden. A group of German tourists filled the place. They were all elderly. A childlike rosiness revealed a network of tiny veins and blood vessels on the men's noses and around their temples; the sturdy legs of the women who resembled the jacks in the Spanish deck of cards displayed the same veiny quality, but the violet knots they formed had a far less innocent appearance. Some of them stretched out on the benches that morning in early November to soak in the last rays of the sun. That setting of grapevines, rosebushes, and tourists stretched out in the sun created an atmosphere as far from an airport as one could imagine. Everything there negated the idea that, within thirty minutes, Dolores, Kyrim, and I would be aboard a device that, in less than an hour, would deposit us along with the blond horde in Samarkand.

Suddenly I was bothered by the intrusion of those men and women, possibly from the Bundes Republik. Everything in them, the noisy laughter, the exploding voices, the clumsiness of their movements, seemed vulgar and therefore repellent. Fifteen hundred years ago, when Bukhara was already a city, the ancestors of those intruders were using their teeth to tear apart the deer that their forests sheltered. Despite the quality of their clothing, the expensive cameras, and the obvious desire to show superiority, their gestures and manners, compared with those of the locals, implied a first in history, something outlandish and deeply garish.

I was overcome by a blind streak of foul humor. It was not just that the presence of foreigners sullied the city; at the end of the day I was one of them even though I tried to convince myself of the notion that deep down we Mexicans were also Asian. What irritated me most was that as I recounted with my two traveling companions, Kyrim and Dolores, the memorable events of the previous night—the nuptial ceremonies we had witnessed—I had blotted out essential details that I reconstructed, and imprecisely at that, only as I listened to their recollection. I tried to hear again the screams, the drums, I tried to visualize the leaps and somersaults of the young people, a clashing red jacket, the crazed, almost parodic steps of a dance, eyes that sparkled because of drunkenness produced not only by alcohol but also by an excitement shared by the multitude; I saw a gold brocade tunic that contrasted with the jeans and modern jackets of most of the celebrants. But the fire, the great bonfire that surely signified, I thought upon hearing my friends' account, a test of purification and vigor, escaped me. Kyrim, who had spent a good part of his life in Tashkent and of the three of us was the only one who knew the region, told us that these ceremonies had nothing to do with Islam but instead harkened back to earlier historical eras; they were reminiscent of the period in which the region saw the zenith of the cult of Zoroaster.

We had left the old city behind. We were walking back to the hotel along a wide avenue and decided to sit down and rest on a bench. I commented I would like nothing more than to attend a theater performance that night; it would be a way, as I watched the spectators and observed their reactions to the spectacle, of experiencing a glimpse of the social fabric of Bukhara. To see how the audience entered, where they sat, how they dressed, which section the adults preferred and which the young people, why and how they laughed, the intensity of applause. I had witnessed this in other places: I had seen a Turkish opera in Ashgabat, a puerile and touching work called *Aina*, and a drama very similar to Faulkner's *As I Lay Dying*, written by a contemporary Siberian author, in a theater of Irkutsk. I had no interest in seeing any Uzbek or Tajik or Russian theater in Bukhara. But how I would have liked to know the reactions of the audience to something more distant, more foreign, *The Merry Widow*, for example; the degraded and marvelously trivialized foam of rituals! To coincide with a tour of the operetta theater of Tashkent, Dushanbe, or Moscow would have been a heavenly experience!

All of a sudden we heard an uproar in the distance, an unexpected howl, a drumbeat followed by an impressive silence. We ended the conversation. In the distance, emerging from one of the barbicans that open onto the walled city, there appeared a group of people carrying torches. Suddenly, the crowd was right in front of us. Two boys and an old man preceded the procession; behind them a group of drums and two or three trumpets of huge proportions; and even farther behind, a motley crowd of about two hundred to 250 people; they were jumping in place as if bouncing on the pavement. The faces and gestures of the dancers were very somber, almost expressionless; they then began to run for a long distance. We stood up and followed the parade. The three dancers (always one old man and two young ones) who were leading the march alternated with others; they danced frantically, swaying in the air, twisting their bodies as if they were about to fall only to rise again before touching the ground, reestablishing a perfect balance. After about one-hundred meters, it bears repeating, they would rejoin the crowd from which a different trio would emerge to play the role of soloists. At moments the procession moved very fast; At others, it crawled at a slow pace, according to the rhythm of the trumpets. Then the drums would roll, and the human mass seemed to be momentarily immobilized; jumping in place, no screaming, their faces almost transfigured by ecstasy. When the immense trumpets began to play again, the crowd gave out a strange kind of roar, something bestial and primitive, an echo born during the earliest stage of man, and then everyone would begin to run, without ever losing the rhythm of dance, only to stop again, listen to the drums, before repeating the whole ritual over and over again. Only the soloists, dancers, and acrobats, who opened the procession, danced without stopping, both in moments of rest and in advance.

We followed them a while, walking beside them on the sidewalk, astonished, surprised, amazed.

Kyrim proposed as a last walk of the night a visit to a park where the ancient tombs of the Samanids were located. We passed through a grove of birch trees. In the distance we could hear the din of the procession, mixed with Uzbek or Turkmen music playing on a radio. There was no one around us. We were the only people walking through that wood. The darkness rendered the tombs invisible. The tales of massacres and mutilations in the alleyways of the old city that Kyrim had recounted earlier began to weigh on us ominously. As we left the park, we once again heard the din and saw the crowd in the distance. The group, it seems, was no longer moving forward. A glow illuminated a low building, wider than the others, but equally blind on the outside, in front of whose door there was a crowd of people much larger than the one we had seen parading.

We walked toward them. The group was no longer advancing but continued jumping and screaming with extraordinary frenzy around what Dolores and Kyrim reminded me the next day was a bonfire. I can't explain how I could forget in just a few hours everything related to that pyre which was the central element of the scene. I could remember, on the other hand, as if they were still in front of me, the intensity of some drunken faces, leaps and somersaults, a fragment of a gold brocade tunic, a scarlet jacket, the monotonous beat of the drum, the shouts, the expression of the young groom, whom they held by the arms and shook to the rhythm of the dance, the placid face of some women who peered from the courtyard where they no doubt safeguarded the purity of the bride. We had returned to the dawn of time. Some unknown intensity repelled me back to earth. I would have liked to jump with the natives, shout like them. When Dolores and

Kyrim told me about the enormous bonfire where the howling mob made the boyfriend jump up and down several times, I was surprised by the partialness of my recollection. How could I have forgotten the fire, have failed to notice it when it was the fundamental element of the party?

As in Jan Kott's treatise on eroticism, the fragmentation of sight could be applied to all kinds of intense sensory experiences. When apprehended by touch, the world disintegrates, the elements separate, are unleashed, and are only perceptible in one or two forceful details that cancel the rest. Why, for instance, a piece of red brocade under a monstrous face? Or a turban, greasy and dirty, and not the bonfire that even now I'm unable to reconstruct with precision? Later, and this I do remember very well, the young groom went through the door beneath a double row of burning torches that formed the canopy of the universe and was delivered to the women who would lead him to the bride. As soon as the wedding cortège entered the house, the shouts and the sound of drums and trumpets ceased, and there was a languorous and undulating music; it was man's leap out of the jungle toward the refinements of Islam. For reasons that are unimportant to relate, we did not accept the invitation extended to us by some young people to participate in the festivities; for me the important thing had already happened.

And it was at the Bukhara airport (as we waited for the plane to take us to Samarkand and the fire was spoken of and I was distressed for having forgotten it) that the old memories that had been trying to flow from the night before began to emerge: the years as a student in Warsaw, the unforgettable conversations with Juan Manuel in the Bristol café, the ways in which we enticed that tiresome, overbearing, and ridiculous painter from whom the whole world fled like the plague to extend her journey through the Soviet nation into Central Asia, Feri's nonexistent adventure, and, above all, an immense nostalgia for lost youth. My hatred for the flock of tourists soaking in the sun broke out again, and for a moment I felt a tiny quiver of unease at our possible involvement in the story of the trip made by the Italian woman to that same region twenty years ago.

"We were not to blame; nothing can make me feel responsible," I said, and I saw that my companions were staring at me, not knowing what I was talking about.

V.

What did we have to feel guilty about? Of the fact that Issa was becoming increasingly more excited about what we were telling her about the exoticism of the places she would later visit, about the artistic vestiges of the past that she would soon discover, about the picturesque customs and the different landscape that she would be given the opportunity to witness? Because it was impossible that she would believe Feri's story, which the young Hungarian pianist invented to distract her, to besot her, to free us at least for a moment from her grumbling, from the list of grievances she made in her lover Roberto Infidel's absence, who at that hour, which we spent chatting in the café, was probably dancing with one of the waitresses whose aura of sweat and beer seemed to attract him so much. Our fault? It would be absurd to think so. Not even then did the idea cross my mind.

The painter's trip lasted three weeks. It was a relief to be rid of her. After the holidays, Juan Manuel returned to Lodz to continue his studies, and I accepted an invitation to spend a season in Drohiczyn, a small ecclesiastical town in southeastern Poland, where solitude allowed me to write and revise stories for a book I planned to edit on my return to Mexico. I had suddenly begun to take literature seriously. I naively believed that from then on I could devote myself almost exclusively to it. One of the stories, with a vaguely Gothic tone, was inspired in part by the figure of the Italian painter; I began by imagining her locked up in a house in that city. The theme was very simple and, as I developed it, I attempted to explain something to myself that usually leaves me speechless when I encounter it in reality: the passion of certain women for repugnant men. The protagonist of this little tale, an Italian woman artist who spends a season in Warsaw, meets a man of Polish ancestry (he could be an Australian or an American), a very primitive sort, morally and intellectually, with absolutely no sensitivity, without family in Poland, but determined to reside in Drohiczyn, the city of his ancestors.

The narrator, who has known the protagonist during an earlier time, encounters her by chance in a restaurant in the old market square, accompanied by a man getting on in years, whose enormous bald head is out of proportion to his insignificant body. He sits with them at the table. This oaf doesn't let anyone else speak. He recounts anecdotes of chilling vulgarity, rattles off a string of stupid remarks on every possible subject, and mocks nonstop what he considers to be his friend's intellectual pretensions. The few words she manages to insert into the conversation are greeted with boorish comments and guffaws from that raging lunatic whose huge bald head at that moment turns red and is drenched in thick sweat.

The narrator, disgusted by the couple, rises minutes later. Even more repugnant than the man's manners is the woman's submissiveness, the beatific expression she wears as she listens to the vulgarities he emits. He is astonished by the couple's moral and mental dissimilarity and the perfect balance they apparently are able to establish.

Years later, while visiting Drohiczyn, he remembers that it is the city that the painter mentioned as her future home. He begins idly, first with reluctance and then with unbridled curiosity, to make inquiries about the couple. A crime has taken place. He would never learn the causes. The end, quite macabre and inexplicable, remains a mere game of conjecture.

Upon returning from Drohiczyn, I phoned Juan Manuel and we agreed to meet in Warsaw. He arrived crestfallen and sullen. He had had during those weeks a love affair with a film student who had been given a prominent role by a famous director in his new film, which overnight had made her a star. He was spending his time in cafés and restaurants on very literary disquisitions about the difference between the reactions of the mind and those of the body at the moment when love ends. All that is accepted rationally, he would say, aware that he wasn't reinventing the wheel, but with absolute conviction, finds its refutation in the senses. A few times it puzzled us that Issa didn't look for us in order to annoy us with her travel impressions. It never occurred to us to look for her.

It was not until one of Juan Manuel's later trips that we ran into Roberto with one of his cheerful barmaids. He was a bit drunk. At first we didn't understand a lot of what he was talking about; after making him repeat the story several times we began to put two and two together. Issa had returned. She was in the hospital. The doctors had told him a very strange story. It seemed that she had been found one morning in one of the Asian cities she had visited, wrapped in a sheet and her body completely mauled, as if a pack of animals had attacked and bitten her; the truth is she was full of holes. She had been admitted to a clinic to treat her wounds and contusions; they then put her on a plane, and when she arrived in Warsaw she had to be readmitted to the hospital. No one understood what she was talking about. She would introduce very strange phrases into the conversation in who knows what language. He had gone to see her twice, but Issa didn't allow him or anyone else close to her bed. They kept her asleep most of the time with sedatives. Her mother and nephew had arrived from Italy to take care of her and take her with them as soon as she recovered. What bothered him the most was that the painter owed him almost four hundred dollars for a leather coat he bought her in Bulgaria, and the family wouldn't even allow him to talk about the matter. This would serve as a lesson, he repeated, not to be so stupid next time and to fish from the local pond.

That was it. We were a bit apprehensive about looking for her. What was the point of visiting her if she couldn't and didn't want to see anyone? We never knew what happened to her or where she had been. I wonder if she actually visited Bukhara. If the ordeal that affected her so strongly had happened there. They took her to Italy some time later and we never heard from her again.

The loudspeaker began to announce the next flight. The Aryan beasts, and we along with them, began to shake off our

lethargy and search for the flight information, to walk unenthu-
siastically to the fence that separated the garden from the landing field.

Moscow, November 1980

THE DARK TWIN

for Enrique Vila-Matas

Justo Navarro writes in his prologue to Paul Auster's *The Red Notebook*: "You write life, and life seems like a life already lived. And the closer you get to things in order to write them better, to translate them better into your own language, to understand them better, the closer you get to things, the more you seem to distance yourself from things, the more things get away from you. Then you grab onto what's closest to you: you talk about yourself as you approach yourself. Being a writer is to become a stranger, a foreigner: you have to start to translate yourself. Writing is a case of impersonation, forging an identity: writing is passing yourself off as someone else."

I recently reread *Tonio Kröger*, Thomas Mann's coming-of-age novel, which I had long since forgotten; I considered it a defense of the writer's loneliness, of the necessary segregation from the world to accomplish the task destined for him by a higher will: "One must have died if one is to be wholly a creator." [1] *Tonio Kröger* is a bildungsroman, the story of a literary and sentimental education. But the divorce between life and creation that Kröger proposes forms only the initial phase of the novel; the result of that education favors the opposite solution: the artist's reconciliation with life.

---

1. Trans. David Luke.

The Romantics abolished all dichotomies: life, destiny, light, shadow, sleep, wakefulness, body, and writing meant for them only fragments of a hazy, imprecise, but in the end, indivisible universe. The exaltation of the body and the passion of the spirit were their greatest desires. The romantic poet conceived of himself as his own laboratory and battlefield. In this story from 1903, Mann incorporated one of the ideals of the period: the idea of ethics as aesthetics, distancing the spirit entirely from all earthly vulgarity. Symbolism is a late offshoot of Romanticism, at least one of its trends. Tonio Kröger is a writer of bourgeois extraction; it fills him with pride to live only for the spirit, which implies a rejection of the world. He fulfills his destiny with the guilty conscience of a bourgeois who is ashamed of the mediocrity of his environment. Hence his asceticism is carried out with almost inhuman rigor. At the end of the novel, following some experiences that connect him to life, Kröger reveals to his confidant, a Russian painter, the conclusion at which he arrives: "You artists call me a bourgeois, and the bourgeois feel they ought to arrest me ... I don't know which of the two hurts me more bitterly. The bourgeois are fools; but you worshippers of beauty, you who say I am phlegmatic and have no longing in my soul, you should remember that there is a kind of artist so profoundly, so primordially fated to be an artist that no longing seems sweeter and more precious to him than his longing for the bliss of the commonplace. I admire those proud, cold spirits who venture out along the paths of grandiose, demonic beauty and despise 'humanity'— but I do not envy them. For if there is anything that can turn a *littérateur* into a true writer, then it is this bourgeois love of mine for the human and the living and the ordinary. It is the source of all warmth, of all kindheartedness and of all humor."[2] End of quote. Tonio Kröger, German writer.

If I confused my recollection of the novel with the image of the writer's total reclusion, his isolation, it is due in no small part to one of his phrases, "One must have died if one is to be wholly a creator," which has been quoted a thousand times as an example of the writer's decision to not commit to anything but himself.

Even if such an attitude is eventually rejected by Tonio Kröger, it is still not surprising to find its echo in Mann's own reflections on old age. His autobiographical pages show his astonishment in the face of his popularity; the warmth with which he is treated by family, friends, and even strangers does not appear to reconcile with the reclusion that was necessary for him to complete his work. The reaction of the elderly Mann is much more convincing than Kröger's final confession, where his love of humanity disguises a declamatory and programmatic tone that fails to touch the depth of the complex relationship between writing and life. "You move away from yourself when you approach yourself...," Navarro says. "Writing is impersonating someone else."

I cannot imagine a novelist who does not use elements of his personal experience, a vision, a memory from childhood or the immediate past, a tone of voice captured in a meeting, a furtive gesture glimpsed by chance, only to incorporate them later into one or more characters. The narrator-writer delves deeper and deeper into his life as his novel progresses. It is not a mere autobiographical exercise; writing a novel solely about one's own life, in most cases, is a vulgarity, a lack of imagination. It is something

---

2. Trans. David Luke.

else: a relentless observation of one's own reflections in order to be able to realize multiple prostheses inside the story.

No matter what, the novelist will continue to write his novel. Never mind that other non-literary works may demand his time. He will focus on his story and will make progress on it in his spare time, on weekends, or holidays, but, even if he himself doesn't realize, he will at all times be implicated secretly in his novel, inserted into one of its folds, lost in its words, pushed by "the urgency of fiction itself, which always carries a certain weight,"[3] to quote Antonio Tabucchi.

I imagine a diplomat who was also a novelist. I would place him in Prague, a wonderful city, as is well known. He has just spent an extended holiday in Madeira and attends a dinner at the Portuguese Embassy. The table is a vision of elegance. To his right sits an elderly doyenne, the wife of the ambassador of a Scandinavian country; on the left, the wife of an official from the Embassy of Albania. The tone of the ambassador's wife is imperious and decisive; she speaks to be heard by those sitting around her. The writer, who has just arrived from Madeira, remarks that he has gotten the better of winter by two months. But he has just begun to talk when she commandeers the conversation to say that the best years of her youth were spent precisely in Funchal. She began her speech not with the city's gardens, nor in the beauty of the mountains, the seascape, the mild climate, nor with the virtues and defects of its inhabitants, but with its hospitality. She declared that tourism in Madeira had always been very exclusive and as an example of refinement commented that at the Reid they served tea with cucumber and butter sandwiches

---

3. Trans. Tim Parks.

on dark bread, as was *de rigueur* in the last century; she spoke at length of her stay on the island where she lived during the war; she said that her father had always been a prudent man, so when the conflict seemed inevitable he decided to move with his family to Portugal, first to Lisbon and later to Madeira, where they settled permanently.

"That is how he was," she continued, "so excessively prudent that we spent five years away from home without our country ever having declared war. It was as if Madeira remained outside the world; correspondence and newspapers arrived with such delay that when news finally arrived, it was already so outdated that one could scarcely be bothered. We settled in Funchal, which goes without saying; where else on the island would we have done so?"

The guests around her ate and nodded; they were only permitted an occasional comment of amazement or agreement, at most a fleeting question that would encourage her to continue her monologue. She spoke of an outing she once took accompanied by her mother to greet countrymen who were going through difficult times. On that afternoon, she wore an absolutely delightful dress of silk chiffon by Edward Molyneux, a combination of lilac flowers on an ocher background and a pleated skirt, which required yards and yards of fabric for its construction. She met that afternoon the man who would become her future husband, making a vague gesture toward the other end of the table where the ambassador, wreathed in a gloomy silence, was seated. For a moment, the writer was perplexed; something in the man's face had changed over the holidays.

"We crossed Funchal until we arrived at a mansion on the

outskirts that had seen better times, on whose terrace lay in deck chairs two youths covered in bandages and in casts from head to toe, taking air; both were convalescing from an accident. They lived there with their parents, a sister, and an English nurse who attended them. They belonged to an old family from my country, yes, the best kind of people, with large sums of money deposited in banks in different countries, although to see them no one would have thought as much; it was a house with little furniture, frighteningly ugly; the garden had become overgrown and where it was not overrun by weeds there were huge holes, like volcano craters."

The dinner guests' attention began to wane. Upon noticing signs of retreat, the old woman raised her voice even more and cast disapproving glances at the deserters, but she was defeated; conversations in small groups or pairs had already spread. Determined, she addressed the writer exclusively, hinting that he should consider it a privilege to hear such intimacies and memories of a place she considered off-limits to strangers.

"I approached the lounge chairs where the young men were lying," she continued, "and one of them, Arthur, quickly raised his partially plastered arm with his free hand, grabbed my big porcelain brick-colored buckle, and pulled me to him, moaning and gasping; the pain from the effort must have been tremendous. 'A sudden outburst of amorous passion,' my mother, who was very wise, commented later. It may have been, but I think the poor, ailing creature was glad to see an impeccably dressed young woman, wrapped in beautifully colored fabrics, since he was always looking at his mother and sister—the nurse does not count—who were dressed like prisoners, which, I can assure you, was almost a crime in Funchal, whose elegance rivaled that of Estoril itself. Ah, such wonderful salons, and terraces, and garden parties! My greatest amusement at soirées was guessing the designers. Who had dressed the Princess Ratibor? Schiaparelli! And General Sikorski's niece? Grès! She was transformed into a Greek sculpture. And the very rich Mrs. Sasseson? None other than Lelong! Yes, sir, Lucien Lelong himself! My mother and I devoted our time at those parties to detecting which was an authentic Balmain, Patou, or Lanvin, and which were copies made by the island's prodigious seamstresses. Those were moments of splendor. One needed the *Gotha* within reach to avoid taking risks; one could be ruined at every step with the central European and Balkan titles. Of Arthur's many wounds the only truly serious one was his knee, which had been shattered in a dynamite explosion. That is why the poor fellow still walks with a limp and not because of sciatica as he would have people believe, much less the bouts of gout as the Finnish doctor has been spreading. Yes, Arthur fell in love with my buckle; he loved the color and asked me to wear it with all of my dresses. It may seem rather immodest on my part, but the belt buckle made him walk again; he began to stand; of course, he fell almost every time, howling in pain; we yelled to him amid applause that nothing could be learned without suffering. Now look at him, he's like a colt! Were it not for me, he might well be prostrate in his deck chair."

At that moment someone interrupted the storyteller, and the novelist took the opportunity to meet the woman who was eating silently to his left. She smiled at him widely and repeated the same words she had said at the beginning of the dinner, which is to say she pointed to her plate and said in broken English, "Is good." It pleased him enormously that a mere two words could make up a conversation because he was deaf in his left ear, and conversations on that side were almost always torture for him; misunderstandings often occurred, his responses seldom coincided with people's questions; in short, it was a nightmare.

The admirer of Madeira once again demanded his attention, and he, to extricate the monologue from the exhausting world of fashion, asked if the two young men had been injured in military action. The woman looked at him sternly and haughtily, and finally answered that the Finnish doctor, not the current but the previous one, had spread a malicious rumor that Arthur and his brothers had exploded the dynamite in order to avoid their military obligation, which was both slanderous and preposterous; none of them feared recruitment for the simple reason that their country was neutral. They had transported the dynamite in a small boat in order to eliminate an islet that was obstructing the view from the house. The oldest brother died, the other was paralyzed for life, and Arthur, the youngest, barely survived. He dreamt of devoting himself to organizing and directing safaris in Central Africa. When he recovered, contrary to what everyone might expect, he devoted himself to studying, and later joined the Foreign Service.

They were now having dessert; the woman from Albania touched his arm slightly, pointed to her plate and said, "Is good," and then, expounding for the first time that night, added, "Is very many pigs," or something that sounded close, and began to laugh delightfully. The wife of the Nordic ambassador appeared insulted. Not wanting to lose her preeminence, she made a comment about desserts in Madeira, especially those at the Reid and the Savoy, but the writer, infected by the gratuitousness of the Albanian woman's humor, suddenly interrupted the ambassador's wife with a comment about Conrad, his travels, and his layovers, and said that he would have liked to know what he said when talking to ladies in Southeast Asia.

"Who?"

"Joseph Conrad. I imagine he must have occasionally received invitations; that he must not have spent all his life talking to merchants and sailors, and that he also spoke to wives, daughters, the sisters of British officials, of shipping agents. What do you think he talked to them about?"

The woman must have thought his deafness had caused him to become lost, and that it was necessary to assist him:

"The Portuguese women dressed with impeccable taste, some in Balenciaga, but their conversation did not always match the *hauteur* of their attire; they always seemed uninteresting to me, not to mention they were also incredibly stingy. They demanded prompt and impeccable work, but for payment they were a calamity. Well, all of them, not just the Portuguese, were dreadfully tightfisted," she exclaimed with sudden bitterness. "The war was a pretext to exercise their greed. They wanted to be queens, and they almost were: princesses, countesses, wives of bankers, in exile, yes, but with their fortunes safe, all of them, without exception, who were unable to appreciate the work that conferred their elegance. They were willing to waste an entire morning in order to begrudge a dressmaker the few escudos needed to survive. Yes, Mr. Ambassador, I shall not take it back: they were all dreadfully tightfisted."

The hosts stood; the twenty-two guests followed suit, and they all moved slowly toward the salon to take coffee and liqueurs and smoke at their leisure. The writer approached, not without a certain morbid curiosity, the husband of the woman to whom he had listened throughout dinner, an elderly man who looked as if he were made of knots arranged haphazardly on bones, a face composed of arbitrarily positioned pits and protrusions, a porcelain prosthetic eye capable of disturbing even the most phlegmatic interlocutor, and a leg that lacked movement. He spoke as intensely as his wife in the presence of two functionaries from the Portuguese Embassy who listened to him dispassionately about the preparations for the upcoming wild boar hunt in the Tatras, which only six or seven very skilled hunters would attend. The writer realized for the first time that he was looking at him with his prosthetic eye, which he always had covered with a black patch. The writer was surprised that the old codger, one-eyed and quasi-paralytic, was awaiting the event with such strange enthusiasm. As soon as he was able, the writer interrupted to say that he had just spent the holiday in Madeira and that he had taken advantage of the time to relax and read. He did not dare add "to write" because the porcelain gaze from the fake eye and the glimmer of confusion that emerged from the real one transformed instantly into a dark horror that bordered almost on dementia. The embassy staff took advantage of the moment to slip away and attend to another solitary guest.

The old man recovered his wits; he asked mockingly, as if he had not heard the writer's words, if he had decided to participate in the boar hunt, if he had oiled his old rifle and counted his cartridges, but, just like his wife, he did not wait for the answer and between groans added that they would leave from Bratislava the following Friday at four thirty in the morning, and that the hunt would last two days. The writer attempted to add that he only went on pheasant hunts, more than anything else because of the accompanying accoutrements: campfires in the snow, hunting music, horns, dinner at the castle. The old man frightened him again as he stared at him with the brutal coldness of his prosthetic eye and the maniacal fury of the other, and just when he expected to be labeled decadent, or "artistic," he was surprised to hear the old man say, his voice stifled, almost unintelligible, that he too had once been to that inferno, that he recalled with horror that abominable island, although the verb *recalled* was perhaps not appropriate, because he never recalled that desolate place, unless someone was foolhardy enough to mention it to him, which, as it were, rarely happened. He was very young then, naive, uncorrupted, you might say; he did not know how to defend himself, much less possess the physical capabilities to do so, when a pack of hungry she-wolves, of she-wolves that were hyenas and vultures, attacked him, beat him with belts and straps, threw him to the ground, bit him, and took advantage of him and his purity. That dark confidence ended with a groan, and then, without saying goodbye, he turned, leapt toward a group of guests most certainly to remind them that the wild boar hunt was to take place next week in Slovakia. He then turned suddenly with military precision, retraced his steps, and faced him once again, as if the conversation had never ended.

"Don't think," he said with an expression marked by sullenness, "that I did not notice my wife's unusual garrulousness at the table tonight. She did not allow anyone to speak, is that not right?

One can never understand women; they spend the whole day immersed in the dreariest silence, and then, when least expected, they turn into magpies. What had her so excited?"

The writer commented that it had been a very instructive conversation; that in an environment as rigid as diplomacy, where women were accustomed to talking about trivialities, it was refreshing to meet a woman who could discuss such interesting topics.

"Topics? What topics?" he asked, as if carrying out a police interrogation. "Answer immediately! To what topics are you referring?"

"Your wife reveled in imagining what Conrad said to European women, the English in particular, in the Malaysian ports. She speculated on how Conrad might describe the dress of those long-suffering colonial women."

"What are you saying, what, about whom was she talking?" It was evident that the response had flummoxed him.

"About the great Joseph Conrad, your wife's favorite novelist."

The old man made a violent gesture with his hand, which could be interpreted as "go to hell!" and he withdrew, hopping like a giant cricket.

Once home, the writer recalled the woman's monologue about her elegant youth in Madeira and her husband's subsequent comments. It seemed as if he had heard two versions of the same highly dramatic situation without having understood much about it, not even what about it was dramatic. And that was precisely the kind of exciting element necessary to create, to begin to invent, a plot. The enigmas were many: a dynamite explosion that takes place on a boat, the absurd explanation of wanting to blow up a reef to improve the view of a house where no one was interested in aesthetics, the couple's relationship, the buckle, the belts, the woman's coldness during this part of the story and, at the same time, the almost crazed excitement with which she described the chiffons and silks and brocades. A few days later, he remarked to some colleagues how strange the encounter with the couple made him feel. He learned that the Finnish doctor had said once that the ambassador's wife had been a dressmaker in her youth, a woman who could reproduce a dress from a mere photograph. He tries to invent a story; the porcelain eye torments him; he begins to imagine scenes and even begins to give them dialogue; the ambition of the dressmaker, spurred by a greedy mother, to trap the suffering boy, heir to a large fortune. He imagines the girl and her mother as third-class guests at some get-togethers, admiring the dresses from the great ateliers of Paris, as well as those they had cut and sewn with their own hands. Whenever they discovered one of theirs they would exchange looks of complicity and joy.

A writer often listens without hearing a word spoken; other voices trap him. The voice of a real person disappears or becomes mere background music. Sometimes a few words send him to one imaginary character or another. Other times—and that's what's so surprising!—the writer doesn't even know that the voices he tries to incorporate into a character, or a plot, are not intended for that story, that lurking under the plot exists another one, waiting for him.

The day arrives when he sits down to work. He has failed to resolve the enigma of the dynamite; he looks for the relationship of the explosive with the craters in the garden of the house in Funchal. Surprisingly, out of the blue, a new character has emerged, a young theosophist who joins the dressmaker and her mother in their daily outings to visit the patient. Sometimes, only the two young women make the visit. Others, the theosophist goes to the injured young man behind her friend's back. The discovery of the young theosophist girl is tantamount to discovering a gold mine. He sees her, hears her, and knows what she's thinking. Her body is very small, her head larger than it should be, but she is far from a monster; at least not physically. There is something about her, however, something frightening: her rigidness, the harshness of her look, her sullen appearance. A fluid contempt for the world seems to exude from each of her pores. The author sees two young women of markedly dissimilar appearance walking down the road that leads to the mansion where the injured man lies: one is blonde and tall, a bit ungainly, well dressed; the other, the theosophist, is wearing a blouse and skirt of an almost military cut. At that moment, she recommends ferociously to the dressmaker something new and wicked to do to the patient. Anyone who saw them would think they were an ostrich and wild boar crossing, without noticing—so lost were they in thought—a flower garden's beauty.

When the novelist finally begins his story, Funchal and its surroundings, all of Madeira and its characters, disappear completely. Only his new discovery, the theosophist, survives. There she is: sitting in a restaurant in the lobby of the Hotel Zevallos; yes, facing the main square in Córdoba, Veracruz, where she moves much more naturally than on the flowering avenues of Funchal, which is not to say that she has become pleasant or polished or relaxed, nothing of the sort. The world is revealed to the writer at that moment. He has begun to translate himself. "Writing is a case of impersonation, forging an identity: writing is passing yourself off as someone else." At that moment, he is now that someone else. By transplanting the location, the young woman maintains her physical characteristics and is still a theosophist. She has returned to her hometown after living with her mother and sister in Los Angeles, California, for twenty years, where the three had feverishly read Annie Besant, Krishnamurti, and, above all, Madame Blavatsky. Upon her mother's death, she travels to Córdoba, which she left when she was six or seven, to claim an inheritance. She stays at the home of family friends, perhaps distant relatives. Everyone knows her as "Chiquitita," a nickname from her childhood and one that fills her with a heavy rage that she dares not show. Her resources are negligible, which is why she doesn't leave the family who has welcomed her; every day she notes her petty expenses in a diary. She has forbidden herself any kind of luxury. A lawyer friend of her mother advises her to contact one of the opposing parties, her Tío Antonio, for example, who is the most amenable. The same lawyer is responsible for arranging the interview. Chiquitita follows his instructions and meets her uncle for lunch one day in the lobby of the Zevallos. He addresses her nonchalantly, as if everything between them were perfect. "What a gorgeous niece I have!" he says as he greets her, adding: "You look much better in person, *caramba*, I mean, what a beauty!" But the young woman at no time lowers her guard; she frowns sullenly throughout the meal. She's the same prickly person she ever was. Watching him drink glass after glass of beer during the meal repulses her. She reprimands him somewhat severely, commenting on the incompatibility of drunkenness and legal affairs. Her uncle laughs, amused, and calls her cutie-pie, kitten, and pipsqueak. At the end, over dessert, her relative agrees to talk about the matter they met to discuss. He insists that he doesn't see the need to go to court, the case should be settled amicably, as should all things among family; that she must, however, understand that the property in dispute does not belong to her, that before leaving Córdoba her mother was compensated appropriately, that while she was alive she received a monthly payment. Just then, he's about to add that in spite of everything the family has considered giving them a sum, the amount of which would be determined when they signed a waiver renouncing their claim but doesn't manage to say it because Chiquitita beats him to the punch. She berates him with a string of disconcerting adjectives and a tone so sarcastic and petulant that the brute becomes enraged and responds with a remark so vulgar that it frightens her. He can be heard shouting, so every local will know, that if anyone in Córdoba remembers her mother, it's because of her whoring around, that he personally would see to it that she and her sister don't see a penny, that he would prove that they were both daughters of someone other than his brother, her mother's husband in name only, and that therefore they had no right to any part of the inheritance. He then adds sarcastically that the best thing she can do is find a husband, or an equivalent, to scratch her belly and support her. Suddenly, the beast of a man gets up and leaves the restaurant. Stunned, Chiquitita remains at the table, not so much because of the violent way she's been treated, or because of the references to her mother's loose behavior, nor because she discovers that recovering the portion of the assets that belongs to her is going to be more—much more!—difficult than she imagined, not even because of the scandal involved, but because of the mere inability to pay the tab. Overcome by rage, and on the verge of tears, she asks the waiter if he'll accept the watch that hangs around her neck for a half hour, the time needed to go where she's staying and pick up the money to cover the bill.

The novelist thinks about his heroine's ensuing movements; he begins to mentally style the language; he imagines he will finish the story in a few days and return to the abandoned plot in Madeira, its characters, the dressmaker (now rid of her theosophist friend), the dynamite explosion, the exercises the injured young man does to regain movement, his falls, the cruel discipline to which he is subjected, unaware that Chiquitita's triumphs and tribulations during her stay in Córdoba would not end anytime soon, that the story he had just started would turn into a novel he would have to live with for several years and where perhaps there might appear a young farmer from Tierra Blanca, Veracruz, who was left paralyzed and blind in one eye mishandling dynamite, and an astute seamstress determined to have him and his property. Over time, the novelist will come to forget that the story came from a dinner at the Portuguese Embassy in Prague. And were the social event ever able to penetrate his memory, he would only vaguely remember an ambassador's wife, probably French, for having unleashed an endless monologue about Parisian haute couture and its most celebrated names. In short, he would consider this incident as one of many moments of diplomatic routine during which he overheard exasperatingly detailed descriptions of locations and situations only to forget them a moment later, and he would never connect it with the appearance of Chiquitita, her misfortunes in Córdoba, and her intrepid fight to defeat—by human intervention, unimaginable tricks, and astral assistance—her enemy relatives until recovering the portion of the inheritance that belonged to her as well as a portion that did not. A novelist is shocked at the sudden appearance of an uninvited character; he often confuses sources, the migration of the characters, the transmutation of karma, to quote Chiquitita and also Thomas Mann, who understood those surprises very well.

The last novel by José Donoso, *Where Elephants Go to Die*, carries an epigraph from William Faulkner that illuminates a novelist's relationship with his work in progress: "A novel is a writer's secret life, the dark twin of a man."

A novelist is someone who hears voices through the voices. He crawls into bed, and suddenly those voices force him to get up, to look for a sheet of paper and write three or four lines, or just a couple of adjectives or the name of a plant. These features, and a few others, cause his life to bear a striking resemblance to that of the deranged, which doesn't bother him in the least; on the contrary, he thanks his muses for having transmitted these voices to him without which he would feel lost. With them he goes about drawing the map of his life. He knows that when he is no longer able do it, death will come for him, not the final death but living death, silence, hibernation, paralysis, which is infinitely worse.

Xalapa, July 1994

BIBLIOGRAPHY OF QUOTED TRANSLATIONS

Kurata, Hyakuzō. Trans. Glenn W. Shaw. *The Priest and His Disciples.* Tokyo: Hokuseido Press, 1938.

Mann, Thomas. Trans. David Luke. *Tonio Kröger and Other Stories.* New York: Bantam Books, 1970.

Tabucchi, Antonio. Trans. Tim Parks. *Flying Creatures of Fra Angelico.* Brooklyn: Archipelago Books, 2012.

SERGIO PITOL DEMENEGHI (1933–2018) was one of Mexico's most influential and well-respected writers, born in the city of Puebla. He studied law and philosophy in Mexico City and spent many years as a cultural attaché in Mexican embassies and consulates across the globe, including in Poland, Hungary, Italy, and China. He is renowned for his intellectual career in the fields of both literary creation and translation, with numerous novels, stories, criticisms, and translations to his name. Pitol is an influential contemporary of the best-known authors of the Latin American "Boom," and began publishing his works in the 1960s. In recognition of the importance of his entire canon of work, Pitol was awarded the two most important prizes in the Spanish language world: the Juan Rulfo Prize in 1999 (now known as the FIL Literary Award in Romance Languages), and the Cervantes Prize, the most prestigious Spanish-language literary prize, often called the "Spanish-language Nobel," in 2005. In 2017, Deep Vellum published *The Magician of Vienna,* the final installment in Pitol's Trilogy of Memory, which includes *The Art of Flight* and *The Journey.* Pitol died in April 2018 at his home in Xalapa, Mexico.

GEORGE HENSON is a literary translator and assistant professor of translation at the Middlebury Institute of International Studies in Monterey. His translations include Cervantes Prize laureate Sergio Pitol's Trilogy of Memory, *The Heart of the Artichoke* by fellow Cervantes recipient Elena Poniatowska, and Luis Jorge Boone's *Cannibal Nights.* His translations have appeared variously in *The Paris Review, The Literary Review, BOMB, The Guardian, Asymptote,* and *Flash Fiction International.* In addition, he is a contributing editor for *World Literature Today* and the translation editor for its sister publication *Latin American Literature Today.*

Thank you all
for your support.
We do this for you,
and could not do
it without you.

DEAR SUBSCRIBERS,

We are both proud of and awed by what you've helped us accomplish so far in achieving and growing our mission. Since our founding, with your help, we've been able to reach over 100,000 English-language readers through the translation and publication of 32 award-winning books, from 5 continents, 24 countries, and 14 languages. In addition, we've been able to participate in over 50 programs in Dallas with 17 of our authors and translators and over 100 conversations nationwide reaching thousands of people, and were named Dallas's Best Publisher by *D Magazine*.

Deep Vellum is a 501c3 nonprofit literary arts organization founded in 2013 in Dallas's historic cultural neighborhood of Deep Ellum. Our mission is threefold: to cultivate a more vibrant, engaged literary arts community both locally and nationally; to promote the craft, discussion, and study of literary translation; and to publish award-winning, diverse international literature in English-language translations.

As a nonprofit organization, we rely on your generosity as individual donors, cultural organizations, government institutions, and charitable foundations. Your tax-deductible recurring or one-time donation provides the basis of our operational budget as we seek out and publish exciting literary works from around the globe and continue to build the partnerships that create a vibrant, thriving literary arts community. Deep Vellum offers various donor levels with opportunities to receive personalized benefits at each level, including books and Deep Vellum merchandise, invitations to special events, and recognition in each book and on our website.

In addition to donations, we rely on subscriptions from readers like you to provide the bedrock of our support, through an ongoing investment that demonstrates your commitment to our editorial vision and mission. The support our 5- and 10-book subscribers provide allows us to demonstrate to potential partners, bookstores, and organizations alike the support and demand for Deep Vellum's literature across a broad readership, giving us the ability to grow our mission in ever-new, ever-innovative ways.

It is crucial that English-language readers have access to diverse perspectives on the human experience, perspectives that literature is uniquely positioned to provide. You can keep the conversation going and growing with us by becoming involved as a donor, subscriber, or volunteer. Contact us at deepvellum.org to learn more today. We would love to hear from you.

Thank you all. Enjoy reading.

Will Evans
Founder & Publisher

PARTNERS

SUBSCRIBERS

Anita Tarar
Anonymous
Ben Nichols
Blair Bullock
Brandye Brown
Caroline West Charles
Dee Mitchell
Charlie Wilcox
Chris Mullikin
Chris Sweet
Christie Tull
Courtney Sheedy
Daniel Kushner
David Bristow
David Travis
Erin Crossett
Fernando Flores
Jeff Goldberg
John Winkelman
Joshua Edwin
Kenneth McClain

Lesley Conzelman
Lytton Smith
Mario Sifuentez
Marisa Bhargava
Martha Gifford
Mary Brockson
Matt Cheney
Merritt Tierce
Michael Aguilar
Michael Elliott
Nathan Wey
Neal Chuang
Patrick Shirak
Samuel Herrera
Shelby Vincent
Stephanie Barr
Steve Jansen
Todd Crocken
Will Pepple

JOSEFINE KLOUGART · *Of Darkness*
translated by Martin Aitken · DENMARK

YANICK LAHENS · *Moonbath*
translated by Emily Gogolak · HAITI

JUNG YOUNG MOON · *Vaseline Buddha*
translated by Yewon Jung · SOUTH KOREA

FOUAD LAROUI · *The Curious Case of Dassoukine's Trousers*
translated by Emma Ramadan · MOROCCO

MARIA GABRIELA LLANSOL · *The Geography of Rebels Trilogy: The Book of
Communities; The Remaining Life; In the House of July & August*
translated by Audrey Young · PORTUGAL

PABLO MARTÍN SÁNCHEZ · *The Anarchist Who Shared My Name*
translated by Jeff Diteman · SPAIN

BRICE MATTHIEUSSENT· *Revenge of the Translator*
translated by Emma Ramadan · FRANCE

LINA MERUANE · *Seeing Red*
translated by Megan McDowell · CHILE

FISTON MWANZA MUJILA · *Tram 83*
translated by Roland Glasser · DEMOCRATIC REPUBLIC OF CONGO

ILJA LEONARD PFEIJFFER · *La Superba*
translated by Michele Hutchison · NETHERLANDS

RICARDO PIGLIA · *Target in the Night*
translated by Sergio Waisman · ARGENTINA

SERGIO PITOL · *The Art of Flight* · *The Journey* · *The Magician of Vienna*
translated by George Henson · MEXICO

AVAILABLE NOW FROM DEEP VELLUM

EDUARDO RABASA · *A Zero-Sum Game*
translated by Christina MacSweeney · MEXICO

JUAN RULFO · *The Golden Cockerel & Other Writings*
translated by Douglas J. Weatherford · MEXICO

MIKHAIL SHISHKIN · *Calligraphy Lesson: The Collected Stories*
translated by Marian Schwartz, Leo Shtutin, Mariya Bashkatova,
Sylvia Maizell · RUSSIA

ÓFEIGUR SIGURÐSSON · *Öræfi: The Wasteland*
translated by Lytton Smith · ICELAND

BAE SUAH · *Recitation*
translated by Deborah Smith · SOUTH KOREA

SERHIY ZHADAN · *Voroshilovgrad*
translated by Reilly Costigan-Humes &
Isaac Stackhouse Wheeler · UKRAINE

FORTHCOMING FROM DEEP VELLUM

GOETHE · *The Golden Goblet: Selected Poems*
translated by Zsuzsanna Ozsváth and Frederick Turner · GERMANY

DIMITRY LIPSKEROV · *The Tool and the Butterflies*
translated by Reilly Costigan-Humes & Isaac Stackhouse Wheeler ·
RUSSIA

DOROTA MASŁOWSKA · *Honey, I Killed the Cats*
translated by Benjamin Paloff · POLAND

JUNG YOUNG MOON · *Seven Samurai Swept Away in a River*
translated by Yewon Jung · SOUTH KOREA

ZAHIA RAHMANI · *"Muslim": A Novel*
translated by Matthew Reeck · FRANCE/ALGERIA

JESSICA SCHIEFAUER · *Girls Lost*
translated by Saskia Vogel · SWEDEN

KIM YIDEUM · *Blood Sisters*
translated by Ji yoon Lee · SOUTH KOREA

**DEEP
VELLUM**